SCIENCE SQUAD

# Hatchling Hero

## A Sea Turtle Defender's Journal

Book design by Jake Slavik
Illustrations by Arpad Olbey

Design Elements: Shutterstock Images and iStockphoto

Published in the United States by Jolly Fish Press, an imprint of North Star Editions, Inc.

First Edition
First Printing, 2018

This is a work of fiction. Names, characters, places, and incidents are either the product of the author's imagination or are used fictitiously, and any resemblance to actual persons living or dead, business establishments, events, or locales is entirely coincidental.

**Library of Congress Cataloging-in-Publication Data (pending)**
978-1-63163-161-0 (paperback)
978-1-63163-160-3 (hardcover)

Jolly Fish Press
North Star Editions, Inc.
2297 Waters Drive
Mendota Heights, MN 55120
www.jollyfishpress.com

Printed in the United States of America

# Hatchling Hero

## A Sea Turtle Defender's Journal

## by J. A. Watson

Illustrations by Arpad Olbey | Text by Courtney Farrell

JOLLY
FiSH
PRESS

Mendota Heights, Minnesota

# Science Squad!

It's official. As of three days ago, I, Clarita Rosita Santiago Romero, am on the Science Squad! Hector joined too. Mamá said it would be good for us to make more friends (I think she really just means *me*), and Tío Gustavo thinks it's time we were "contributing members" of our local community (whatever *that* means). According to Tío, that's what makes America so great. But really, I think they just wanted us to have something to do now that it's almost summer vacation. I swear, my mother listens to all Tío's advice since we moved to North Carolina to live with him. AND HE'S HER LITTLE BROTHER. I can't imagine ever doing that with Hector!

But if I'm being honest, I'm not that upset about the Science Squad. I like science, and the kids seem nice, so I'm sure it will be all right. Who knows? Maybe Mamá will be right. Maybe I will finally make some friends here!

But anyway, tomorrow is our first meeting. We are supposed to decide on a direction for the project we were going to do over the summer. I wonder what we'll pick.

# Our First Meeting

I went to my first Science Squad meeting after school today! Besides me and Hector, the other members are Emily, Danny, Jennifer, and her little sister, Janey. This is what they look like:

Emily Grant

Danny Lewis

Janey Chen

Jennifer Chen

We did a little get-to-know-you, and I found out a few things.

## WHAT I LEARNED:

- Emily loves butterflies and hummingbirds and anything cute. But she's super into spiders too! Ew.
- Danny is the smartest of all of us. He has more education stickers than anyone.
- Jennifer and Janey Chen are sisters. They sort of remind me of me and Hector because Jennifer, the older sister, is pretty much perfect in every way. And her little sister is annoying.

Haha! I only wrote that because Hector was just looking over my shoulder.

But really, I think Science Squad is going to be a good thing for me. The truth is, it was really hard for me when we first moved here. I spoke differently than everyone, and kids at school seemed to have all the friends they wanted already. At lunch, they sat in such tight little circles, I couldn't have wedged my body between their shoulders if I wanted to. Some kids made fun of my Spanish accent; the rest mostly ignored me.

*Maybe with the Science Squad it will be different . . .*

*But anyway, the "objective" (that's the word Danny used) of our meeting was to figure out what we were going to focus on for our summer project.*

*Emily read a list of options: We could help monitor air pollution, collect and index fungi, track the spread of invasive plants . . . Nothing really jumped out at me until she said something about leatherback sea turtles. We would see sea turtles all the time ~~back home~~ in Puerto Rico, but I didn't know they were in North Carolina too!*

*"Sea turtles? What about sea turtles?" I couldn't help myself. I don't usually speak up like that—especially around people I don't know. But that's the project I wanted to do. It reminded me of ~~home~~ Puerto Rico.*

*Emily smiled. "Well, it looks like there are a couple things we could do with sea turtles, mostly having to do with observing them or tracking them . . ." She trailed off while she continued to read to herself. "Guys, I like this idea. What if we did our project on sea turtles?"*

*Everyone murmured their agreement.*

*So, we're doing our project on sea turtles. We still have to find a mentor for our club, someone who knows a lot about sea turtles or marine life and can help guide* us. The old mentor, Mr. O'Leary, was a geologist. He told us to start looking for someone new.

But, at least we have our project figured out. I am SO excited.

# The Day the Kaiju Came

Last night, I was sitting on the porch outside our house when a huge, dark shape crawled from the water. The shadow dragged itself up the beach. I sat up straight. My heart pounded out of my chest. It was a sea turtle! A huge black one! Her shell was longer than I am tall. The turtle had a lot of trouble moving up the sand. That's when I saw fishing line tangled around her right front flipper, pinning it to her body. She could hardly walk. We had to help her!

I jumped off the porch and yelled for my brother to come quick.

Hector came running, sand flying behind him. In the light of the moon, the turtle looked like a giant blob. Hector stopped just before he reached me, his eyes wide. He took a few steps backward.

"Kaiju!" he screamed.

Kaiju are made-up monsters from those Japanese films that Hector loves. They aren't even real, and I've told him so. (I think my brother watches too many old Godzilla movies.) I told him to just calm down and follow me. We snuck closer, and I showed him that it wasn't a monster. It was a sea turtle, all tangled up in fishing line. I sent Hector into the house to get the scissors.

Hector took one more look at the giant turtle and sprinted inside. I slowly crept closer to the turtle. The turtle made deep grunts as she made her way up the beach. She was trying hard. But the fishing line was making it difficult to move. My knees started to shake. She was seriously HUGE.

She had to be in pain. I could see in the moonlight how the fishing line had cut into her skin. Her flipper was trapped, but she kept trying to move it. Every twitch tugged thin, strong fishing line farther into the cut. We needed some good, sharp scissors to cut the line and free her. Where WAS Hector?!

I saw a light go on upstairs. In Mamá's sewing room.

Uh-oh. Hector was taking Mamá's scissors?

We aren't supposed to use Mamá's special sewing scissors. Not on paper, not on anything. I guess it went without saying that using them to cut fishing line off a giant sea turtle was not okay. I knew that. I didn't

12

forget. But I forgot to remind Hector of that when he jumped off the porch stairs with the sharp end of Mamá's scissors pointed right at me.

"HECTOR!" I yelled. "Don't run with scissors!"

Hector made a face at me. He does that a lot. "Hurry, hurry! Come quick," he said in a high, girly voice. I think he was pretending to be me, even though I do NOT sound like that. "But don't *run* or anything."

He tried to hand me a flashlight but I shook my head. "We can't use that," I whispered. "The bright light will confuse her."

"Oh yeah. Right," he said. He tucked the flashlight into his back pocket. My little brother actually looked a little frazzled, which was unusual for him. He doesn't ever seem afraid, even when he should be. I swear, some days it's like he thinks he's bulletproof or something.

We both crept closer to the turtle to get a better look. Her back was a mottled brown, green, and black, with white spots like a starry sky. She had a short neck and small eyes. And she was humungous.

Hector whispered something and pointed at the fishing line. I couldn't hear him over the sound of waves crashing on the beach, but I got the idea. We had to get that fishing line off. Somehow, we had to get it out of the cut on the turtle's flipper too. Hector pushed the scissors at me. I leaned back, palms out, and shook my head. We had a stupid whispered argument. For some reason, we both whispered, even though the turtle didn't seem to notice us. She inched up the beach like she was on a mission.

We were wasting time. I grabbed the scissors from Hector's hand and slowly made my way to the turtle. I crouched down, picked up a handful of fishing line from the turtle's flipper, and started snipping. If Mamá saw me with her sewing scissors, she'd be mad. But she loves animals, so maybe that made the scissor-stealing okay?

Plus Mamá wasn't home. She was at night class (she's going to be a nurse!). And my uncle was gone too, leading a night-fishing trip. That is why I was babysitting my brother. It's been this way since we moved here from Puerto Rico. It's often just Hector and me on our own. Babysitting him isn't the worst thing ever (he is nine years old, after all), but sometimes his crazy ideas get us into trouble.

*Tick-tick-tick.* I kept snipping at the fishing line, slowly following alongside the sea turtle as she inched her way up the beach. At one point, the turtle kicked a spray of soft, damp sand onto my bare arm. It tickled my skin. I handed fistfuls of tough, wiry fishing line to Hector as I cut. If we left it on the beach, other animals might get tangled in it.

One last snip and I had the largest tangled piece of fishing wire in my hand. Her right flipper came free with a jerk. It was long and pointed, perfect for swimming. Not so good on land. But with two flippers, the turtle moved faster. I put the scissors down and wiped my forehead.

"Well, at least she can move freely now," I said to Hector.

We watched the turtle crawl up the beach to a shadowy spot. There was still fishing line in that cut—we could see a couple inches of it glisten in the moonlight. I didn't see how we'd get the remaining wire out of the wound, not with the turtle using both flippers at once to scoot up the beach. I remember the sounds of shifting sand that came on the wind. For a minute, I wasn't sure what I heard. Maybe just the waves?

I willed my eyes to see into the shadows, wondering what she was doing over there.

15

"I think she's digging," Hector said.

"Why?" I asked.

"Well, Clarita, because that's how you make a hole," he said real slow, like I was stupid.

He thinks he's so funny.

We wanted to give her space, so we went to sit on the porch swing and watch. We could see her a little better from there anyway. Her movements were slow, but sure enough, she was digging a hole. She slowly scooped sand up with one back flipper and moved it off to the side. Then she used the other back flipper and did the same thing. I wondered if she was digging a nest.

It wasn't long before Hector fell asleep. Awake, my little brother is loud and annoying. Asleep, he's kind of cute. But I would never tell him that.

After sitting there for a while, watching the turtle's dark shape slowly dig, I took out my phone to check the time. I shook Hector awake.

"Mamá will be home soon," I whispered to him. "We should get inside."

"Huh?" was all he said.

"Get up, you lazy bones," I said. That did it.

"But what about the turtle?" he asked.

We tiptoed over to see what she was doing. Round, white eggs slid out of her hind end. The eggs looked like ping-pong balls, only slimy. So I was right! She WAS digging a nest to lay eggs! This is what it looked like:

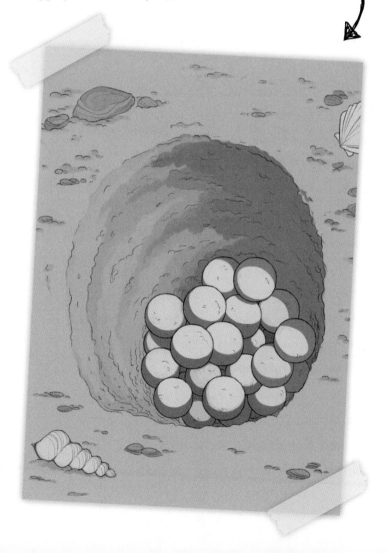

We knew she would go back to the ocean when she was done laying eggs. After all, you don't see giant turtles hanging around the beach every day. But what if the mother turtle left and still had fishing line around her flipper? What would happen to the baby turtles without her? What kind of mother leaves her babies behind, anyway?

Hector crawled right up to the giant turtle. He must have decided the turtle wasn't Kaiju after all (even though it had a beak that looked like it could snap your finger off). While she was busy laying eggs, he grabbed the last strand of fishing line and yanked it out with his bare hands. The huge turtle flinched, and I jumped back. I almost peed my pants!

Anyway, we did it! Our turtle could swim freely again!

In related news, Hector and I are grounded. We managed to get in bed before Mamá got home, but may have forgotten ONE thing in our frenzy to do so . . .

This morning, before Mamá left for work, we took her outside to show her the sea turtle nest. The nest isn't that exciting. It just looks like a dug-up patch of sand. You can't see any eggs because they're all buried. But Mamá found her sewing shears in the sand where I set them down last night. Hector tried to tell her we were saving lives, like superheroes. Mamá said we can put on tights and a cape anytime we want, only we'd better save lives with the *old* utility scissors—not her nice new ones. So we're stuck at home for a few days. No está bien.

That's it for now. I took a couple pictures with my cell phone as the turtle crawled back to the water. I can't wait to show the Science Squad.

# The ~~Three~~ Six Things I Learned

This morning I scouted up and down the beach and found nothing but broken seashells. No giant sea turtle in sight. Mother sea turtles really do go back to the ocean and leave their eggs all alone. What terrible mothers! Good thing they lay so many eggs. I bet this nest has at least a hundred! I wonder how many of them will survive?

Hector compared the cell phone pictures I took of the turtle to photos online, and he decided the turtle we saw was a leatherback. I think he's right. I looked up leatherbacks and learned three things:

1. They are one of seven species of sea turtle. According to the IUCN (International Union for Conservation of Nature) Red List of Threatened species, they are considered "vulnerable."

2. Leatherback sea turtles have a very wide range. That means they swim in oceans and nest on beaches all over the world, except where it's frozen.

3. Leatherback sea turtles don't have a shell covered in hard keratin as other turtles do. Rather, the bony plates that make up its shell are covered by a leathery skin. Their backs have seven pale, raised ridges.

I edited a picture I took last night so it was brighter. All sorts of things showed up! I could see the raised ridges on the turtle's ~~shell~~ back. The ridges on her back show up clearly in the picture. I also noticed a little box on top of her shell. The box looks man-made: there's a wire coming off it, and there are numbers written on it.

I went online to find out about the box (I wonder if it's some sort of tracking device? Are scientists tracking this turtle?). But, of course, I got distracted and started to read about other turtle stuff. I found out three more cool things about leatherback sea turtles:

4. They are the largest species of sea turtle. Most of

them are four to eight feet long, and they weigh 500 to 2,000 pounds.

5. The biggest one ever recorded was found dead on a beach in Wales after drowning in a fishing net. Sea turtles can hold their breath a long time but not forever, so they can drown if they get trapped underwater. The dead turtle was almost nine feet long and weighed a little over one ton. The article said the turtle was 100 years old, but I don't really know how they could tell.

6. Leatherbacks have been around since the time of the dinosaurs! They were doing fine until people started messing up the oceans. Plastic trash is a huge threat to sea turtles. Apparently, sea turtles eat floating plastic, especially plastic bags and balloons. I guess to a turtle, plastic bags and balloons must look a lot like jellyfish.

## Note to self:

Pick up trash on the beach at least once a week!

Sea turtles are threatened by floating plastic in the ocean. Eating plastic will block a turtle's digestive track, and that can be deadly. Plastics are petroleum based. Plastic trash will never biodegrade. When something biodegrades, it gets broken down into soil. Once-living materials, like banana peels, can biodegrade. Plastic does not. It just breaks up into smaller pieces as it gets churned by waves. Floating trash can threaten sea turtles and other ocean animals forever.

# Age Is Just a Number . . .

Okay, so that sea turtle in Wales was nagging at me. How could they possibly know that it was 100 years old? I decided I had to do some more research.

Turns out, scientists use a method called skeletochronology to determine a sea turtle's age. (This is how you say it: Skel-e-toe-chron-ol-o-gy.) Basically, it means that scientists use a turtle's skeleton to see how old it is.

When I told Hector about it, all he said was "cool."

He's so annoying sometimes. But even though he was acting uninterested, he had stopped watching superhero cartoons when I was talking. I took that as a sign that he wanted to know more.

I told him how scientists look at the humerus, which is a bone in the flipper. You have to look at the actual bone though, so you can't do it on a live turtle. Rings of bone are added each year, kind of like tree rings. But scientists have found that the method doesn't work very well in leatherbacks. So maybe that Wales turtle wasn't 100 years old (or maybe it was older!).

"I wonder how old our turtle is?" Hector mused.

I had no idea, so I guessed. "Maybe fifty or sixty, from her size." (She was as long as our kitchen table!)

"That's ancient," Hector said. "Kind of like . . . you."

"Hector!" I screamed. "I'm only twelve."

"Almost thirteen." He grinned. "Ancient."

Little brothers are such a pain.

# The Embarrassing Truth

We had another Science Squad meeting today, and Hector and I told everyone about our late-night visitor. Everyone was super excited, and Emily even high-fived me when I showed her the pictures I took.

They all made me promise to take a video of the hatchings as they, well, hatched. I promised I would. It will be great for our research!

There's only one problem . . . I don't know how to make a video on my new phone.

When we got home from the meeting, I sucked it up and admitted the embarrassing truth to Hector.

"That's because old people are not good with technology," Hector laughed. (He really needs to stop that joke. It isn't funny anymore.)

He proceeded to jump off the couch, snatch my brand-new cell phone out of my hands, and run for his room. The door slammed and locked.

That happened hours ago, and he still has my phone. He'd better be careful with it. He's just jealous because Mamá bought one for me and not him. I only got it because I have to babysit him while she's at school and Tío's at work. She says it's "for emergencies." I'm pretty sure Hector stealing my phone doesn't count as an emergency. Good thing, because if it was, I don't have the phone to make a call on!

Anyway, leatherback eggs take about sixty days to hatch (sometimes it's longer!). So I have about two months to figure out the video thing on my phone. Until about mid-July. I can hardly wait! I'm going to mark my calendar.

# What That Box Is For

Turns out, I was right! Scientists ARE tracking my turtle. (I've decided she's mine, even if we don't hang out very often. Hector is just gonna have to deal with it. Ha!) I did some research and found out that the box on her back is a tracking device. Biologists are using it to track *my* turtle. The wire on top is an antenna. The box talks to a satellite, so they can track her wherever she goes.

I've been wondering who exactly is tracking my turtle. So I posted a message on the Science Squad message board. It's a board for just Science Squad members and mentors. Here's my message:

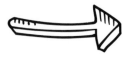

–

 Science Squad HQ > Message Boards

### C. Romero
ONLINE NOW

Hey Science Squad kids and mentors!

I need some help! My brother and I have a leatherback sea turtle nest on the beach behind our house. We saw the turtle dig the nest (after we saved her from some nasty fishing line!), and I noticed that she had a tracking device on her back.

I'm wondering if anyone is tracking a leatherback turtle on North Carolina's coast?

In only an hour, I got a response from Dr. Angela Samuelson. She works as a veterinarian at the Wildlife Rehabilitation Clinic here in North Carolina. She and other researchers she works with have been tracking my turtle! But that's not all. The best part is she's also registered to be a Science Squad mentor, and she offered to mentor our club. Mr. O'Leary is going to meet with her to make sure she's a good fit and has all the credentials to be our mentor.

I hope it works out because it'd be perfect!

Leatherback turtles migrate farther than any other species of turtle. They can travel 10,000 miles per year, searching for food and mates. They are able to sense ocean currents, chemistry, and Earth's electromagnetic fields to direct their migration routes. Standard migration routes take the turtles to all sorts of places, including North Carolina, around May of every year.

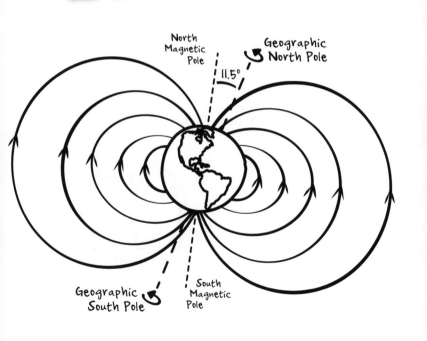

# STICKERS!

Today when I logged on to Science Squad HQ there was a new sticker on my profile page. I earned it for posting about sea turtles! There are different kinds of stickers: research (which is what I got), education (if you teach others about something important), and action (for taking actions like cleaning up the environment or protecting animals and plants). Danny has more stickers than me, and Emily has LOTS more. But they've been in Science Squad longer than I have, so I'm okay with that.

Anyway, GO ME!

# Dr. Angela Samuelson

I'm starting to like journaling. It helps me make sense of everything. Right now, I'm so excited, I don't even know where to begin. Dr. Angela Samuelson is officially our mentor! And she was at our meeting today. She is about twenty-five years old, and she just graduated from vet school. She's smart and nice and everything I want to be when I grow up. Except blond. I'll never be blond like her, at least not without a lot of bleach.

She knew who I was when we met, and she said nice things about my research on sea turtles. She's planning to come to our beach to look at the nest.

Dr. Angela invited our Science Squad to visit the Clinic next week. They have a sea turtle hospital there. The Clinic also takes in injured and orphaned wildlife, like raccoons and fawns. I can't wait to visit. Hector says he wants to hold a raccoon. Not me. What if it bites?

# ~~My~~ Our Turtle and Her Nest

Today, Dr. Angela and some biologists from the Clinic came out to check on the turtle nest. It was so fun.

The biologists stuck a long tool they called a probe down into the sand and checked the temperature inside the nest. They took a lot of notes and said that so far, the nest looks good. Dr. Angela and her team put up signs warning people that a nest is on this beach and that it shouldn't be disturbed. The signs look like this:

· KEEP OUT ·

Nest of an Endangered Leatherback Sea Turtle. Bothering the nest or their eggs is ILLEGAL.

I overheard Dr. Angela and the biologists talking about how lucky it was that this nest was still undisturbed. I learned that some turtle nests in our area have been found dug up. Dr. Angela wasn't sure why. Maybe animals were looking for yummy eggs. Or maybe there are poachers around. Eek! I sure hope we don't have any poachers around here! Because I think leatherback turtles are amazing.

## Reasons leatherback turtles are amazing:

1. Leatherback females make more than one nest in a summer. That's so if one nest is destroyed somehow, there are still babies born from other nests.

2. The mother is long gone by the time the eggs hatch. The babies are on their own from day one. Most of them die. A few will grow up to be ocean giants that live for 100 years (or more!).

3. Seagulls and crabs snap up baby turtles when they hatch. Those who make it to the ocean face other predators, like big fish. That's why sea turtles lay so many eggs.

*Anyway, the other cool thing that happened is that Dr. Angela gave me a link to the website where I can track the mother turtle! I went online, and she (the turtle, I mean, not Dr. Angela) is swimming around just offshore.*

*Hector was super excited when I told him we might see our turtle again. (Okay, I guess she can be OUR turtle instead of MY turtle.) I also told Hector I'm a little worried about her. I didn't know that there could be poachers around, trying to catch her. Usually I don't share worries with my brother. I'm afraid he might make fun of me. This time, he didn't laugh at all. And he actually offered to do research with me. So we did it together, which was fun.*

## Things I learned about turtles:

- During the summers, mother turtles hang around near the shore in places called inter-nesting habitats. (I had to look that one up. *Inter* means between, so inter-nesting is where they stay between making nests.)

- Leatherback turtles lay seven to eleven clutches of eggs every nesting season.

- During that time, mother leatherbacks come on shore about once every ten days to dig nest holes in the sand and lay eggs.

- Sea turtles face danger everywhere they go. When they come to the surface to breathe, sea turtles are sometimes hit by fast boats. It's lucky they lay eggs at night because most of the boats are gone by then.

*Now I'm worried about our turtle. It's only May, so chances are she's not done laying eggs yet. What would happen if she tried to come back to this beach and one of those big beach parties was going on? Beach parties happen all the time in summer around here. People come here on vacation and for weekends. They like to party on the beach late at night and make a lot of noise. Dr. Angela says that sometimes people ignore the signs about not disturbing the nest. I hope nothing happens to our turtle or her nest!*

# Notes on Commercial Longlines

. . . And now I have more reason to worry about ~~my~~ our turtle. In Hector's research, he found that our turtle will be in more danger when she leaves the inter-nesting habitat at the end of summer and goes back out to sea. There are a lot of dangers to turtles out in the ocean. One of them is being caught on commercial longlines meant for big ocean fish like tuna.

Commercial longlines can be miles long. Boats pull them through the water. The lines have thousands of hooks, all baited with species such as squid, mackerel, and sardines. When turtles try to take a bite of tasty squid, they get a hook in the mouth. Some turtles bite off the sharp hooks and might swallow them. That can damage their insides. Turtles can also get caught on the hooks and trapped underwater, where they drown. One study estimated that sixty *thousand* leatherback sea turtles die on commercial longlines every year.

41

I keep thinking of our turtle, swimming out there undefended. I hope she isn't one of sixty thousand that don't make it. I wish there was more I could do.

# Sea Turtle Defenders, Unite!

We had another Science Squad meeting after school today. Hector and I told the team what we learned about turtles and all the dangers they faced.

Leatherbacks are an endangered species. That means there aren't very many of them, and they are in danger of going extinct. When a species goes extinct, the very last one has died. They are gone forever, and they are never coming back. Like the dinosaurs! I told the Squad we can't let that happen to our turtles.

Then Hector jumped in. He said we should fight for them, like superheroes, defending the weak. Hector may be obsessed with superheroes, but I think he's right.

Emily, Danny, Jennifer, and even Janey agreed.

We decided we are going to protect those eggs until they hatch!

Hector suggested we call ourselves the Sea Turtle Defenders.

The Squad was quiet for a moment before Danny said, "Yeah, I like that." Turns out, everyone else did too.

That's right. We're the Sea Turtle Defenders. And we'll do whatever it takes to help sea turtles.

# Raccoons!

Oh my gosh, you will never believe what happened. Two nights ago, a family of raccoons came and tried to dig up the sea turtle eggs. Talk about a tasty midnight snack! Luckily, Baxter, our neighbor Mr. Carter's dog, chased them off. Hector gave him a leftover sausage to say thanks. I mean, Hector gave the sausage to *Baxter*, not to Mr. Carter. Ha! Old Mr. Carter probably wouldn't take a cold sausage out of Hector's grubby hand. Anyway, the eggs are three weeks old now. About six more weeks to go! I don't think I'll be able to sleep until they're hatched. I'll be a zombie by the time they finally emerge.

# We Built a Barricade!

*Funny how last time I wrote, I said was turning into a zombie. Well, I think the transformation is almost complete. I'm going to get no sleep tonight, yet again. A bunch of college kids are throwing a party as we speak on the beach right outside our house. Mamá is at class (again), and Tío is fishing (again), so I am alone with Hector.*

*It all started when a crowd of college kids built a bonfire and started getting loud. They totally ignored the signs about the nest. Carloads of college girls showed up. Loud electronic music thudded through our walls. Then a trailer pulled up and unloaded four ATVs. Guys drove up and down the beach like crazy, skidding and spinning circles.*

*Hector wanted to get outside and defend the turtle nest. He was afraid the eggs were going to get squished. I fidgeted by the window, trying to make up my mind. I* didn't know what to do. I almost called Dr. Angela, but I thought she might be asleep.

The Red Cross babysitting class I took said to avoid strangers. The responsible thing to do was to stay in the house. But how could we be sure those ATVs wouldn't crush the eggs? Were they buried deep enough that they'd be safe if somebody drove right over them? I didn't know.

Then I had an idea. "Let's build a barricade." We ran outside and piled up our bikes and a bunch of porch furniture around the nest.

Then I made Hector go back in the house with me. I locked the doors, and now we are watching through the window. The barricade is working great. Every pass down the beach, the ATVs have to swerve around the pile of junk—and around the turtle nest. The party is still going on, but at least the turtle eggs are safe.

# Back to Reality

This morning, I woke up to the sounds of clanking
and banging on our porch. Hector was outside, throwing
garbage into our big metal trash can. I went out and
found a giant mess on the beach. Blackened, burned
wood still smoked. Bottles and cans lay all over the sand,
along with plastic food wrappers. I snatched up the
plastic first, before it could blow into the water. Hector
hauled the plastic recycling tote out onto the sand and
started loading cans and bottles into it. Last of all, we
dumped a bucket of seawater onto the still-smoking fire.
Together, we carried the heavy recycling tote back to
the house.

Mamá met us at the door, wanting to know what had happened. I told her there was a big party last night, with nobody we knew, but that we stayed out of it (which was mostly true). Mamá said she was proud of us that we'd cleaned up the beach even though we didn't make the mess.

Then she noticed we'd left our bikes outside. That got us the usual lecture about how long she'd saved to buy us those bikes and how unlocked bikes can get stolen, blah, blah, blah. I really love my mom. But sometimes she says the same thing over and over. It's annoying, even if I know she's right.

Hector made it worse when he blurted out that we needed our bikes for the barricade. Our mother's eyebrows went up. That was always a bad sign. We took her outside and showed her what we'd done to protect the turtle eggs. Mamá frowned. Cue lecture numero dos.

I hear it all the time. It always starts with the same thing: Clarita should have known better. This time, "Clarita should have known better than to take Hector outside with strangers all over the place." The lecture went on FOREVER.

Mamá was right, of course. I do feel bad about letting Hector go outside last night. I take babysitting seriously. But the turtle eggs were important too! Her lectures always ended the same way: "Remember, never talk to strangers."

"Yes, Mamá," I said.

"We weren't talking to them," Hector muttered under his breath. "Just cleaning up their mess."

I know Mamá is right. We *shouldn't* have gone out there last night. But we did it for a good reason. We needed to protect that turtle nest!

After Tío Gustavo woke up, I heard them talking in the kitchen. They were speaking in Spanish and trying to keep their voices low, but we heard enough of what they were saying. She was worried about all the partying going on right outside our door.

Hector did his best Mamá impression. He waved his hands in the air and talked in a fake high-pitched voice. "Kaiju! Kaiju are everywhere! I never would have left Puerto Rico if I knew it would be like this."

I had to laugh. Hector's Mamá impression was great!

Our neighborhood isn't really a bad one. I just think Mamá feels bad about being gone so much. So she makes up for it by being overprotective when she is home.

I gave her an extra hug at lunch, just because.

# The Fence and the Secret

After that beach party, Hector and I decided we needed a better barricade around the turtle nest. Those eggs needed a real fence. We talked to Dr. Angela, and she thought it was a good idea. She said it was something that the Science Squad could do. She gave me some instructions to share with the group. So, just like that, it was up to the Sea Turtle Defenders to build a fence!

I pried my phone out of Hector's hands and texted the Science Squad. Emily and Danny said they'd come over and help. Jennifer and her sister Janey were out of town, visiting family someplace.

Danny and Emily rolled in on their bikes just in time to help us find fencing. We started in our garage. It was dusty and pretty bare—at least of anything we could use for a fence. Then we started to walk the beach to look for driftwood we could build with.

Mr. Carter walked by with Baxter and asked us if he could help us find anything.

Hector told him we were building a barricade around the turtle nest. Turns out Mr. Carter likes sea turtles. In a minute, he came out of his garage with a roll of bright-orange plastic fencing. We all thanked him at once. That made Mr. Carter smile so wide, we could see the gold teeth in the back of his mouth.

Danny and Hector dragged the roll of fencing to our house. Working together, we all fenced off the turtle nest and posted a few more of our own signs warning people to stay away.

After we were done, we started racing each other up and down the beach. We caught up to a couple guys, a big one with a Panthers baseball cap and a skinny one. The skinny one was carrying a five-gallon plastic bucket. It looked like it was heavy.

Hector ran up and tried to peek into the bucket, but the big one stepped in his way. He laughed and told Hector that whatever was in the bucket would make them a lot of money.

The skinny guy told the stout one to shut up.

I think Hector was going to say something else, but Danny pulled him away and suggested we all head back to our house.

When we got back, Mamá and Tío were drinking iced tea on the back porch. Our mom offered us some lemonade. Then us kids sat on the stairs together and pretended to enjoy the ocean view. But we were *really* spying on the two strangers.

At one point, they whooped and high-fived after looking in that bucket. They were pretty excited about whatever was in there. Why was it such a big secret? I don't know, but I'll tell you one thing: I'm going to keep an eye on those guys.

The Endangered Species Act of 1973 was a huge step forward for animal conservation efforts. It includes a list of 2,270 endangered species. One hundred fifty-seven of those are local to the United States, and it is the government's responsibility to regulate and protect them. The bill includes guidelines on how to bring species back from the brink of extinction. Not only does it make the hunting of rare species like sea turtles illegal, but it also includes guidelines for protecting their wildlife habitats and breeding them in captivity to eventually be released back into the wild. Finally, the Endangered Species Act encourages nations to work together toward a mutual goal of protecting and conserving animal life.

# Stolen!

So my first year of school in America is finally over. I am so excited for summer vacation, especially now that I've got the Science Squad.

Today, Hector wanted to play soccer, so we invited the whole Squad over. I'm so glad that I have my Science Squad friends! But we needed a few more kids to play, so we rode our bikes a few blocks over to find Trent and Carl, two boys my brother knew from school.

When we got to their house, I wasn't sure we had the right place. The house was old and weathered. A broken freezer lay on its side in the weedy front lawn. The screen door hung on by one hinge at a crazy angle. Tires, trash, and cigarette butts were strewn all over. Our house is old too. We don't have much money, and our house needs paint. But at least we use trash cans. I thought about what it must be like for Trent and Carl to live here. Maybe they lived with just their mom or dad who was often away at work? Hector and I are lucky to have both our mom and our uncle to help with things around the house. I know it was hard for my mom back in Puerto Rico before we moved here and in with Tío.

No one answered when Hector knocked on the door. But as we were turning to leave, a skinny, sunburned boy in a tank top came around from the back of the house. Turns out, it was Carl. He gave Hector a half-hearted fist bump and told him sorry, he couldn't play today.

Carl told my brother how he was helping his neighbor, Bobby, who had "business to take care of." So he had to stay here to "keep things under control."

But then Hector begged, like he always does. Hector told him it would be for just a little bit. That was when things got weird.

Carl said, "Can't. Bobby has me keeping my eye on some weird eggs. I have to make sure nobody comes to steal the eggs. He says they're super valuable, and some people might try to take them if they think nobody's home."

*Eggs? What eggs?* I thought. I had a sinking feeling in my stomach.

Then Carl asked us if we wanted to see the eggs. He said they had a whole bucketful.

Hector asked what kind of eggs and where Carl got them. Hector looked at me sideways, and I knew he wanted to see the eggs as badly as I did.

Carl said he didn't know what kind they were. I wasn't sure that was true, but I didn't say so.

Then Carl said the eggs came from someplace outside. On a beach.

Danny and Emily started whispering like crazy. Then it hit me. Could Carl's neighbor, Bobby, be one of the guys we saw leaving the beach with that white bucket? Were there turtle eggs in that bucket?! If we took pictures, we could prove that Bobby stole them from a nest. And then Bobby might get in all kinds of trouble. Maybe even Carl too. I realized I was getting ahead of myself. Maybe there weren't even turtle eggs in that bucket. They could be chicken eggs from a farm. But why would someone need to guard a bucket of chicken eggs?

We couldn't do anything without proof, anyway. The Squad all looked at each other. I decided to speak up.

I causally said, "Sure, we'll take a look at those eggs."

We followed Carl up to the front door. I peeked inside through the broken screen door. The place was a mess. The cat litter box by the door looked like it hadn't been cleaned in a long time. The fumes made my eyes water. Empty bottles stood on a low coffee table in front of a sagging, stained gray couch. The kitchen table was overflowing with newspapers and empty food containers. Flies buzzed around a pile of dirty dishes in the kitchen sink.

Carl opened the refrigerator and pulled out a white five-gallon bucket. He hauled the bucket to the front door and shifted it in his hands to open the door. I could see a few grains of golden sand clinging to the outside of the bucket. Sand, exactly the color of the sand on our beach.

He tilted the bucket toward us, and I held my breath as I inched closer, still unable to see inside. I pulled my phone from my pocket and hid it behind my thigh. This was it! I glanced down and switched it to camera mode. Just a little bit closer and—

Just then, a shiny white pickup truck with huge lifted tires rumbled up the driveway and stopped. It looked strange, all new and clean, parked in that junky yard. Carl flew into the house with the bucket. He slammed the refrigerator door shut just as a tall, skinny man stomped onto the front porch.

It *was* the same guy we had seen on the beach! And that *had* to be the same bucket.

"Carl, what's goin' on here?" the man, Bobby, demanded. "You know I said you ain't havin' nobody over! All you kids, scram! Carl, go git me that bucket back."

Carl ran to grab the bucket he had just put back in the refrigerator. The rest of us didn't need to be told twice. I grabbed Hector's hand. Jennifer grabbed her sister, Janey. We all jumped on our bikes and raced down the street. We got back to our house in record time, all shook up and out of breath. Everyone forgot about playing soccer.

At first, we just stared at each other in shock. After we'd all calmed down, we started asking each other questions, like if we thought there had been stolen turtle eggs in that bucket.

"Ask questions, seek answers"—that's the Science Squad motto. We asked a lot of questions but still had no answers. We promised each other we would find out.

We checked our turtle nest, just to be safe. I breathed a sigh of relief when I saw that it looked untouched.

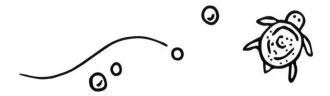

# Visit to the Wildlife Rehabilitation Clinic

Today was the day the Science Squad got to go to the Wildlife Rehabilitation Clinic! At the Clinic, veterinarians help sick animals get well. Dr. Angela met us at the door and showed us around. Everybody there was so nice.

Right inside the Clinic, it's like a museum, with displays about local animals. Lots of tourists visit and give donations. The vet clinic part is in back. Cages hold wild animals that have gotten sick or hurt. On the covered porch outside, they have big aboveground swimming pools, like the kind some parents set up in backyards for their kids to play in. Only these pools have injured turtles in them.

We got to look at them. One loggerhead turtle had big gashes across its shell from when a sharp boat propeller hit it. Another turtle was missing a flipper. It

63

can't survive in the wild, so it will have to live in a tank forever. I felt sorry for it.

All along the coast, there are speed limits for boats. That keeps sea animals from being hurt by fast-spinning boat propellers. But some people go too fast anyway. That's rotten of them. Luckily, lots of turtles at the Clinic are getting better. They will get to go free.

One turtle we saw is healed. And Dr. Angela invited the Science Squad and our families to go along on the boat when they release it! It's a young Kemp's ridley turtle, and its shell is only about a foot long. The Clinic biologists said it is big enough to be safe from many ocean predators already, except for sharks. The Kemp's ridley had a bad cut on a flipper, but it is all better now. In a few days, we will all go on the boat to find a safe place to release it. The turtle will wear a transmitter, which is an electronic device that sends a signal to a satellite in orbit around the Earth. Then we can track it. Tracking helps scientists learn more about the species and what they need to survive.

At the Clinic, we saw a different turtle with a big lump on its face. Dr. Angela said it had a disease called fibropapillomatosis. (You say it:

Fi-bro-pap-ill-o-ma-toe-sis). Scientists call it FP for short. Turtles with FP have tumors on their faces and bodies. Tumors are lumps of tissue that grow where they shouldn't. The sick turtle I saw was a green turtle. Apparently, green turtles are the species most likely to get this disease. One tumor covered most of an eye, so the turtle couldn't see very well on that side. The vets will do surgery on it to remove the tumor, and after that, the turtle should be fine. FP has been found in leatherbacks before too. I hope our turtle doesn't get sick!

The Wildlife Rehabilitation Clinic had lots of great photos on the walls. One whole series was about the dangers to sea turtle eggs. In North Carolina, raccoons, wild hogs, coyotes, and ghost crabs all eat turtle eggs. Some people eat them too! I can't imagine that. Why would anyone want to eat a turtle egg?

# POACHERS!

Something scary happened last night. It was evening, and Mamá and Tío were gone—this time to the grocery store. Hector and I were supposed to stay inside until they got back. But we heard Baxter barking next door. He almost never barks. I peeked out the window to see what was going on. Just then, two dark shadows passed our porch light. The shadows stopped, and I could tell from the outlines they were men. They started to pull on the plastic temporary fence around the nest. They were after the eggs!

I called to Hector and told him somebody was messing around with the turtle nest. Hector dropped my phone. It takes a lot to get him to let go of it, but that sure did it. He yanked open a drawer and grabbed our biggest flashlight. We ran to the window. Hector shined the light on the intruders. It was those same guys: Carl's neighbor Bobby and his friend! Bobby had a shovel.

Hector banged on the window and yelled at them to get away. I told my brother to stay inside. I tried to sound like a boss, but my voice came out high and scared. Not very boss-like. Luckily, he made no move toward the door.

Through the open window, we could hear the men talking. One of them said we were "only kids."

I watched the big one pull the sign off the fence and throw it to the ground. Then they both wrestled with the plastic fencing, trying to pull it away from the nest. The big one got it loose and threw it alongside the sign.

"Thanks, Jason," Bobby said. He started for his shovel.

We started screaming out the window for them to stop. I was so mad and scared, I don't even remember everything I said. I do remember shouting that I was calling the police, and they were going to jail. The men didn't seem to know what to do. But they hadn't actually started digging.

I ran for my phone, but before I could call Mamá or 911, Tío's Jeep pulled in the driveway. He was back—with Mamá!

We ran to the driveway, shouting at them to help us save the eggs. We were practically hysterical at that point, and they led us inside to sit down.

"There's no time to sit!" I yelled. "Poachers are stealing our turtle's eggs!"

That got through to them. Tío ordered us to stay inside, and he went out the back door onto the beach alone. Mamá called after him to be careful.

We were nervous with Tío out chasing egg poachers. Mamá sat on the couch and put her arms around me and Hector at once. I could feel her shaking. But when she got up to call the police, her voice was calm. I was kind of impressed. That reminded me, so I grabbed my phone and sent a message to Dr. Angela: "*Poachers!*"

Tío came back shaking his head. He had looked everywhere, but the poachers were gone. All our frantic screaming must have scared them off.

Soon, a police officer was on our doorstep. I gave her the poachers' names and a description, and she made notes.

Then, Dr. Angela and another biologist (Brian) from the Wildlife Rehabilitation Clinic showed up to check on the nest. The scientists dropped their thermometer probe into the sand, looked at the numbers on the little screen, and sighed. Nobody said anything to us, but Hector and I both knew something was wrong. They spread sand back over the nest and put the fence up again.

When Dr. Angela came back inside, her blond hair was all windblown and messy. She told us the temperature had dropped in the nest. The eggs weren't uncovered for long, so it might stabilize again. *I hope the turtles are okay!*

Tío asked if they wanted to sit, and he offered them some coffee.

Dr. Angela looked at him appreciatively and said, "Thank you, Gus. That would be nice." And then blushed.

*What was that all about?*

Having them there was nice because we got to talk with Dr. Angela and Brian, and it helped take my mind off the poachers. Then Brian told us some things about turtle nests that I didn't know.

## THREE THINGS ABOUT TURTLE NESTS:

1. Temperature affects the gender ratio (the number of males compared to the number of females).

2. Warmer temperatures equal more females, and cooler nests equal more males.

3. If it gets too cold, the eggs may not hatch at all.

Dr. Angela and Brian said they thought this nest would probably be fine. They thanked me and Hector. Dr. Angela even hugged me before she drove away. That made me feel better.

I texted the Science Squad and told them everything. They are super worried about us and the eggs, even though I told them we were safe.

Hector wanted me to tell the Squad that we would defend the baby turtles like superheroes. There we go with the superheroes again.

"Like superheroes?" I asked.

Hector didn't even crack a smile. "Yeah. Like superheroes."

So I sent another text like Hector asked. The Squad sent back cheering emojis. Emily suggested we get security cameras, and put some up on the nest and more around the house. We can't afford them, but maybe Dr. Angela's clinic could.

When we were done texting, Hector said something that I won't forget: "From now on, we guard that nest."

"Right," I said. "And we've got the Science Squad to back us up if anything happens."

We fist-bumped and went upstairs together. For the first time, I felt like we were a team.

The leatherback population is declining at an alarming rate, partially because of how many people poach them for eggs, meat, and organs. In some cultures, turtle meat is believed to have medicinal properties. But eating turtles can spread infections like salmonella, and it harms an already endangered species.

# Superheroes

So I know I'm hard on Hector and his obsession with superheroes, but honestly, it's just because I love him. The kids at our old school sometimes made fun of him for being into superheroes. But those cartoon heroes mean a lot to Hector. He pretends to be like them. I see him try to be brave when he's afraid. And he always wants to stand up and fight to protect the innocent. Just like we're doing for the turtles.

So anyway, I guess sometimes I give him a hard time in hopes that other people won't. That's a little backward thinking, I know. I just don't ever want him to feel left out. I've been in that position before, and I wouldn't wish it on anyone, especially him.

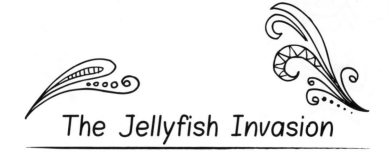

# The Jellyfish Invasion

Dr. Angela thought Emily's idea of security cameras was a good one. After checking with Mamá and Tío, people from the Wildlife Rehabilitation Clinic came out first thing this morning and set them up.

Hector and I played on the beach while that was going on. We got out our boogie boards and rode the waves. It was great! I didn't get a single jellyfish sting. Jellyfish float in the water like upside-down bowls. Many species have long, transparent tentacles that hang down below them. If you touch one, it stings! That's how jellyfish capture their food. Jellyfish wash up on the beach sometimes, and on the sand, they are hard to see. If you step on one barefoot—ZOW! You can get stung. Dr. Angela says there are more jellyfish around than there used to be. That's because of climate change. The oceans are warming, and warm water carries less oxygen than cold water. Fish do worse in warm, oxygen-poor water, and jellies do better.

# A Ride on the Catamaran

This afternoon was the day we got to help release the Kemp's ridley sea turtle! The whole Squad came, and some of their parents too! Mamá came with us. We rode on the Wildlife Rehabilitation Clinic's big boat. It has two hulls and is called a catamaran. I rode right up front, lying on my belly. I pretended I was a dolphin, dancing over the waves. The sea air smelled cool and fresh in my face, and blue waves splashed and thudded against our boat's shiny white hulls. My T-shirt got damp from the spray, but I didn't mind.

The Kemp's ridley turtle rode on deck in a plastic box. Biologists put towels damp with seawater over his back to keep him comfortable. He kicked his fins in the box. Maybe he was getting ready to go home.

We stopped in a quiet bay, with no houses or roads nearby. The biologists let everybody see the turtle one last time as they attached the transmitter to its shell. The device is called a platform terminal transmitter, or

PTT for short. Whenever the Kemp's ridley turtle comes up for air, the PTT will send information to a satellite orbiting in space. The PTT helps scientists find out things like where the turtle goes, how deep it dives, and what the water temperature is.

The catamaran had a back deck, low to the water, so divers could get on and off. We had to stay in the boat, but the turtle didn't. Everyone cheered as Dr. Angela and Brian lifted him from the box and set him free. He swam away on the surface, so the antenna of his PTT stuck out of the water. I imagined it sending its first signal to a satellite, soaring high above us in space.

The turtle looked strong and healthy as he disappeared into the ocean at the edge of the salt marsh. I think he'll be all right.

I was so happy to see him go. I think my mom was happy too. The wind blew through her dark hair, and she had a huge smile on her face. I'm glad she was able to come with us today. She's been so busy with school and work lately.

As the boat turned around and headed for home, she leaned down and whispered that it looked like I had made some good friends through Science Squad. I smiled because I knew she was right.

When we got home earlier this afternoon, the turtle nest seemed fine. The orange plastic temporary fence with our warning sign was still in place. Nobody had messed with it.

Hector was tired, but I wasn't. I logged on to the turtle tracking website. I typed in the numbers from our mother leatherback's ID tag, and she showed up as a little dot moving along the shore. She was only about ten miles north of us!

# And This Day Shall Go Down in History . . .

Today, while Mamá was at work, we hung out with Tío. Hector used MY phone to show us his Science Squad profile. For his profile picture, he posted a funny shot of himself flexing his skinny biceps like a strong man. Hector and I both have three stickers now. We earned an action sticker for cleaning up the beach, but the big surprise for us both was the sticker we earned for education. If enough other Science Squad kids click on your link and read your post, that counts as educating others. Then you win an education sticker. I got one for my post I wrote about sea turtle nesting. And Hector got his for his research on salt marshes.

Using my phone—again, or rather, still—Hector showed Tío how we track our mother leatherback by satellite. We were super excited to see that she was exploring the coastline nearby. Maybe she was ready to dig another nest! Hector begged Tío to take us out on his skiff so we could see our turtle again.

"We can track her on my smartphone while we're out," Hector said eagerly.

"I think you mean *my* smartphone," I said, shooting him a dirty look.

Then I told Hector that it probably wasn't the best idea. Following wild animals around isn't good for them. We are friends to the mother leatherback turtle, but she doesn't know that. Having loud boat engines nearby might stress her out. That wouldn't be good. Especially if she was trying to nest.

"You're probably right," Hector said.

That was a first. I'm recording it here so I can always remember this day—when Hector thought I was right for once. Ha!

# Secret Agent

This morning, Tío took Hector and me to breakfast at the Oceanside Café. The whole place smelled wonderful, like bacon and coffee and pancakes. We sat outside on their deck, under bright red umbrellas that fluttered in the sea breeze. Our breakfast burritos were cheesy and delicious.

The whole time we were there, Hector was on my phone. As usual. He managed to eat his whole meal without putting it down for a second. I swear, he spends more time on my phone than I do. Using the restaurant's Wi-Fi, he kept looking at the turtle tracking site.

As he looked at our leatherback's migration route, he noticed that the mother turtle had come ashore on the beach late last night, just north of our house. I was excited.

"Do you think she dug a new nest?" I asked.

Hector said he didn't think so. The tracker showed that she was only on shore for a few minutes. The last time she laid eggs, it took hours.

I wondered what that beach looked like. Leatherbacks won't nest on beaches that are covered with garbage and fallen branches because it makes digging too hard. Maybe she checked out a beach and didn't like it.

Then Tío told us that there had been a hurricane in North Carolina a couple years ago, before we moved up here to live with him. The wind had knocked down trees and dumped debris on the beaches. A lot of it was probably still there. That reminds me . . .

## Note to self:

Get the Science Squad to that beach soon to clean it up.

"What if she doesn't find a good place to nest?" Hector asked. "What will happen? Will she pop? Will the eggs hatch inside her?"

I laughed and told him it would be okay. Our turtle would find a nesting spot. I just hoped she'd find a good one.

At the table next to us, a man with dark sunglasses looked up when I laughed. I could have sworn he was staring right at me, like he knew me. I looked away. Something about him gave me the creeps. I scooted a little closer to Tío.

The man's phone rang, and he picked it up. As he talked on the phone, he got angry. His voice boomed across the patio. "That's the price. Take it or leave it. I've got other buyers if you don't want 'em."

Hector nudged my elbow, and my eyes went wide. Suddenly, I knew where I'd seen that guy. It was Carl's neighbor Bobby, the egg poacher!

Bobby kept talking on the phone. "Meat? Um, I guess. Sure, if the price is right. I hear it makes good soup."

Hector and I exchanged horrified glances. Was he talking about turtle meat? Would that guy really kill a sea turtle for money? He could go to jail for that!

Tío told us to quit staring. It wasn't polite. We both looked away.

I got up and said I needed to go to the bathroom. I really didn't need to. What I needed to do was find out what Bobby was up to. What I needed to do was to act like a secret agent.

I cut behind Bobby's chair. A laptop computer stood open on his table. I snuck a peek at the screen. He had the turtle tracking site up. That's how he was finding nests! I almost ran back to our table and blurted that out, but I stopped myself. I had to act casual.

So I strolled to the bathroom and took my time washing my hands afterward. Then I went back to my seat without even glancing at the him. I was *so* smooth—I don't think he even noticed!

Back at our table, I said we needed to leave the restaurant. Tío told me to sit back down. We hadn't even gotten our bill yet. I huffed impatiently and sat down.

After what seemed like hours (but was probably only a couple minutes), we paid and left the restaurant. The second we got out of earshot, Hector and I both started talking at once. We told Tío that the guy that was sitting next to us was a poacher. I told them he was using the turtle tracking website to find nests! I also said I was afraid he was going to kill the mother turtle for meat.

Tío told us to slow down. Hector and I were talking over one another and he was having a hard time understanding what we were saying.

We walked to the edge of the parking lot where we could just see the patio out back of the Oceanside Café. Hector pointed to the skinny guy in the sunglasses. Tío frowned when I told him that was one of the guys we had seen outside our house that night when the turtle nest got dug up. And that I had just seen his computer, and he had the turtle tracking website up. That's how the poachers were finding the nests.

Hector's face darkened with anger. "That website is for people who love sea turtles. Not people who want to profit from driving them extinct."

We begged Tío to help us. If he took us out in his skiff, we could track the turtle and intercept the poachers. Even as we said it, I knew that was no solution. The poachers could always come back later and find the nest. We couldn't follow the poachers everywhere. What were we going to do?

"You can't take the law into your own hands," Tío explained. "I'm going to call Dr. Angela. She might have an idea what we can do about this. Clarita, why don't you call the police."

I'd never called the police before. I was so nervous, my palms were sweating!

Hector hates being left out, so he plastered his face against mine, trying to listen in. Strands of his straight black hair got caught between my lips. Yuck! I put the call on speaker just to make Hector back off. The dispatch lady asked me about the nature of my emergency, and I told her about endangered sea turtles and egg poachers and the poacher named Bobby. I offered to take her to his house. I could find the place, even if I didn't know his address.

The dispatch lady's sigh came through loud and clear on the phone. I could tell she didn't take me seriously. She said unless there was an ACTUAL crime being committed, they couldn't do anything about it. I said there *was* an actual crime because the man had eggs in a bucket, even if I never exactly saw inside the bucket. Huge fail. All I got out of that phone call was a promise that there would be extra patrols along the beach that night.

Hector and I walked down the beach to where Tío stood talking to Dr. Angela on the phone. He had a silly grin on his face and quickly turned away from us as we approached. Was Tío sweet on Dr. Angela? She was awfully pretty. And smart.

When Tío finally got off the phone, it was all business. "Niños, I don't think this is something we should get in the middle of. We've alerted the police to the possibility of poachers, and we've got a camera on the nest. That's the best we can do."

No amount of arguing could convince him otherwise. That was it. Hector and I slumped back to Tío's Jeep, defeated. We were supposed to be Sea Turtle Defenders. But it seemed like there was nothing else we could do.

On the way home, we checked the turtle tracker again. Our turtle was still in the area, just a few miles north of our house. And she had moved closer to shore. Did that mean she was getting ready to make another nest? Dr. Angela told me that turtles usually mate and nest on the same beach each time or very close to it. And our turtle wasn't far away from the first nest now.

I checked the map. If our turtle came straight to shore, she'd land on a remote beach surrounded by swamp. Hector looked over my shoulder, biting his lip. I could tell we had the same thought. If we knew where our turtle was, so did Bobby.

Hector and I exchanged a glance. We knew exactly what we needed to do.

I texted the Science Squad. We needed to get the Turtle Defenders together for a rescue!

# The Night Mission, Part 1

You wouldn't believe the trouble we got into last night! After this morning, we knew Tío wouldn't take us out in his skiff to rescue the turtle. So we didn't even bother to ask him. Because if we never asked him, we weren't *technically* disobeying him if we found a way to get there ourselves, were we?

Even though I think my cool secret agent act at the restaurant was stellar, Hector has a lot of secret agent potential too. It was his idea to get permission for the Science Squad kids to do a sleepover at our house. That was the easy part. Tío was home tonight, and he thought it sounded like fun. (I also think he was happy to see us making new friends.)

The plan was that once we got ourselves to the swamp (more on that later), we'd check if the mother turtle was nesting. If she was, we'd watch over her and her nest. If we saw any poachers, we'd text Dr. Angela, and she'd be able to contact the police for us.

The plan was relatively simple, but it turned out
to be anything but. And Mamá would freak out if she
knew what really happened. But I keep getting ahead of
myself. Let me start at the beginning . . .

Emily and Danny were in for our sleepover. Jennifer
and Janey had some family in town and couldn't come.
We planned to do a campout on the beach, right outside
the house. We made a big deal out of hauling camping
gear outside and getting our supplies in order. But while
Tío wasn't looking, Emily and I stashed the small tent in
his skiff, which was tied to the neighborhood pier. Then it
was time to transform ourselves into secret agents.

Hector and Danny went into Hector's room to get
dressed. Emily and I went into mine. Our eyes met, and
a thrill of fear shivered through my chest. We planned
on being out all night, and there might be poachers!
Emily said she had butterflies in her stomach. I did too.
I told her we were secret agents for all sea turtles,
not crime-fighting superheroes—no matter what Hector
thought. If we witnessed a crime, then we could call the
police. Otherwise, we'd stay out of it.

But I wondered out loud if Hector was right.
"Actually, maybe we *are* superheroes. Only not in tights,
please. And no capes."

Emily grinned. "We're the Turtle Defenders! Fighting
crime—but not in tights."

We laughed.

The idea of us as crime-fighting superheroes made
my heart skip. I swallowed hard. "Secret agent" sounded
less dangerous. Either way, there was no going back now.

I sorted through my closet. "Hmm. What does a
secret agent wear on the job?"

Black, I decided. All black. I pulled on long,
lightweight black running pants that fit disturbingly like
tights. Emily noticed and snickered. I groaned.

I added a lightweight, long-sleeved black jacket with
a hood. The long sleeves made me sweat, but I needed
them as armor against mosquitoes. There were billions of
mosquitoes in the swamp.

A knock sounded at my door. I opened it. Hector
stood there, in his own black running pants. Okay, *tights*,
if you insist. And his were even tighter than mine. He was
wearing his Superman shirt. I didn't say a word about

that. Whatever it took to get him through the night. His eyes were bright, and I could tell he was nervous too.

*Good,* I thought. Maybe then he won't take any stupid chances, like running out to fight poachers in the dark.

My brother tossed a can of bug spray into my duffle. I managed to croak my thanks. I was so nervous, my mouth was dry. I packed the flashlights, and Hector handed me my phone. It felt slick and cold and unfamiliar in my hand. The battery was full. He'd planned ahead. Good kid.

Emily and Danny had brought food and water for us all. That was part of the plan. It kept us out of the kitchen and out from under Tío's nose.

"Do you have a jacket for when we're out on the water?" I asked Hector. Somehow, talking made me less afraid. Or maybe I was just putting off the inevitable moment where we get in the boat and there was no turning back.

"Yeah. I packed my black one." He looked at me in my all-black secret agent/superhero suit, and suddenly, we were both giggling.

*Black. Good, we'd be invisible.* The smile slipped from my face. I pulled my little brother into a hug and whispered fiercely in his ear, "This really is dangerous. Don't do anything stupid out there. If they commit a crime, against eggs or turtles or anything, we get it on video."

Then I realized I STILL didn't know how to do that.

After we pulled away, Hector read the admission on my face and put his hand out for my phone. He thumbed it to the camera icon, then swiped sideways for video. All I had to do was hit the red button. Easy as that.

We shouldered our duffle bags. Then Hector, Emily, Danny, and I marched down the stairs. I wondered if superheroes ever felt like this. Sick and scared and thrilled to be on an adventure, all at once.

We faked smiles the second we saw Tío. He couldn't see us looking scared, or he'd know we were up to something. My pasted-on grin felt a little stiff around the lips. I hoped he didn't notice.

"Tío, we're going to play some hide-and-seek before we camp," I told him. It was sort of true . . .

Tío glanced up from the TV, told us to have fun, and went back to his show. I was surprised he didn't even bat an eye. Was he really that dense? Should he really be in charge of us? I felt a little bad for ~~lying~~ not telling him the whole truth, but we did promise to defend the sea turtles. So at least I was trying to do SOMETHING right.

Outside, the sun was going down, and shreds of blood-red light splashed the horizon. The sky turned that beautiful shade of blue you get right before everything goes black. I hoped that wasn't a bad omen. We half-heartedly played some hide-and-seek, the boys against the girls, while we waited for the sky to grow completely dark.

When it was time, we all ran as quietly as we could to the end of the small neighborhood pier, where Tío's skiff was waiting. It was just an open-top rowboat with an outboard motor, but it would work for what we needed to do.

We stowed our duffle bags and stepped into the small boat. That was when I had to make my confession to the group: I didn't *actually* know how to drive the boat. But thank goodness Danny did. He sat in back to man the tiller. The skiff rocked as we settled ourselves in, which did nothing for my nervous stomach. I sat on the middle bench with Emily and let Hector have the front. The air was muggy. Sweat stuck my shirt to my back underneath my life preserver.

Danny fired up the motor, and we headed north. We didn't know what we were getting ourselves into when we set out. That gave us a couple good hours before everything fell apart. When we left the harbor, my biggest fear was getting my phone wet. If I'd known what would happen that night, I might have jumped overboard, phone and all, and swam back home to my comfy bed.

# The Night Mission, Part 2

It started out so slow, so calm. Roller coasters do that too. And then the screaming begins. The skiff chugged north, past miles of salt marsh. Danny took his time, which I appreciated. But the salt marsh was muddy, muggy, and full of mosquitoes.

When we left our house far enough behind, Hector switched on a light on the prow. We weren't lost, even if it felt that way. I navigated, going between a marine mapping app and the sea turtle tracking site. We followed the coast north. Our mother leatherback's signal came from a cove just beyond the salt march. The perfect place for a nest. At least, I hoped.

We entered shallow water at the edge of the marsh. Danny slowed way down to weave between sunken logs in the water. Then the bugs caught up with us. The rotten smell of swamp gas rose up all around us, and mosquitoes buzzed in my ears. We fought back with bug spray, but the little vampires still tanked up on my blood.

I kept watching my brother. He was so tense! I knew he'd been studying the salt marsh, so I asked him to teach us about it. Mainly, I just wanted to distract him.

Hector's voice sounded small when he told us about the salt marsh and the network of freshwater streams that flow across big, muddy fields of grass called spartina. Spartina is special because it can live in salty water. Extra salt gets squeezed out onto the surface of the leaves.

"So if you licked one, it would taste salty. I thought that was . . . cool," Hector said. His voice trailed off, and he shrank down on his bench seat. His head turned from side to side as he tried to pierce the darkness with his eyes. I felt sorry for him. It seemed like he'd been doing better when he was talking, so I tried to keep him going. I knew some of the marsh around there had been drained to build houses (I had read his article on the Science Squad HQ, after all), so I asked him, "Why don't they do that anymore?"

Hector said it was against the law. Salt marsh is important because most of the fish and crabs we eat breed there. Babies of all different kinds hide in the salt marsh until they get strong enough to face the open ocean. Plus, wetlands filter muddy water that comes from the shore. Silt sinks out there before it smothers the coral reef. (Yes, there are coral reefs in North Carolina! I was surprised. I thought they were only in warm, tropical locations.)

I asked why the marsh had so many mosquitoes. He told us that mosquitoes breed in stagnant water. And they were important for the ecosystem because lots of animals eat them.

We had reached a point where the turtle's signal came from just offshore. By then, we'd made it through the salt marsh and could see a sandy beach along the shore.

"We're here," I whispered to Danny. "Turn off the motor and we'll row in." I wanted to make sure we didn't hit our turtle.

Danny nodded in agreement, and Hector switched off the light on the prow, leaving us in sudden darkness. Were we the only ones here? I hoped so. But if not, we definitely didn't want to be seen. I resisted reaching for my flashlight. Something about the dark was unnerving. In the dark, every tiny noise sounded like thunder to my ears. Water splashed softly, and crickets chirped.

Somewhere off to our left, a red fox screamed. Foxes can make the weirdest noises, like women in pain. The foxes did nothing for my pounding heart.

The cove was beautiful at night. Moonlight reflected off the water, making the pale sand gleam. Hector, Emily, and I jumped out of the skiff and unloaded our gear, piling it up on shore. Then Danny hid the boat in some tall beach grasses. The back of my neck prickled then, and I wondered who was watching us. Hopefully, just a rabbit or a deer. Whatever it was, I didn't like it. Because if we could track the sea turtle out there, poachers could too.

I faked a brave smile for Hector's sake. "Maybe our turtle will pick this beach to nest on. It's not too far from the other nest."

Hector barely answered. His eyes kept flicking from side to side, into the shadows. "Yeah. Hope so."

We all helped haul the camping gear a little way inland. I stumbled over roots and rocks. Once, I was unable to catch myself, and I fell, biting my lip against the pain from my scraped knee. I shook it off.

When we finally stopped, the air felt cooler. The heavy scent of some night-blooming flower filled the air.

We pulled the tent out of its nylon duffle. A bewildering jumble of stakes and tent poles thudded onto the ground. After some confusion and frustration, we got the tent up. We were exhausted by the time we finally crawled inside the musty-smelling tent and unzipped the windows, leaving the screens up to keep out the bugs. The only light came from the bright little screen of our phones. We unrolled sleeping pads and sat on top of our lightweight sleeping bags while Emily cheerfully handed out apples.

I munched on one while I checked the turtle tracking website. Our leatherback was still in the ocean, right offshore. Time ticked past. Hector yawned and nodded, then sank down into sleep. My eyelids grew heavy. Emily whispered that she'd take first watch. She'd watch the tracker and wake us all up if the mother leatherback showed up.

She didn't have to tell me twice. I slept, dreaming of turtles soaring through undersea gardens, flapping their fins like wings.

I was jolted awake by a loud rumble. It was late, and the full moon shone through the mesh window overhead.

Emily lay slumped next to me. She must have drifted off while keeping watch.

"Psst, Emily," I whispered. "Get up. Do you hear anything?"

The rumble of a boat engine grew louder, and men's voices, shouting. "Pull up here. I got it right on the map. It's onshore. Gotta be layin' eggs."

Emily looked at me pale and wide-eyed.

"Hurry up. Get the net!" another man yelled. "Whoo-hoo! We're in business."

We shook Hector and Danny awake, and I started shoving my feet into my tennis shoes. We had to keep quiet. The poachers were here! A bright spotlight swept the shore. We flattened ourselves as the beam passed over our tent.

We gathered our things as fast as we could. This mission was to get the poachers on video, and do it without being seen.

We slipped out the open tent flap. Hector went first. Dressed all in black, he almost disappeared into the shadows. I had to be at least as hard to see. I bent over and tiptoed after him. Emily and Danny followed. *We're safe. No one can see us. We're safe,* I repeated to myself. My phone chimed as a message came through. I jumped, and Hector said something that sounded an awful lot like a bad word. I yanked my phone from my pocket and silenced it. It was Janey Chen, on her sister Jennifer's phone.

"It's Janey," I whispered to the others. "They're worried about us."

"I'm worried about us too," Hector snapped under his breath.

We crouched behind some bushes. The strangers' boat was a lot bigger than ours. Bright lights beamed from all around its deck, and it had a mechanical winch for raising heavy crab traps. A boxy wheelhouse jutted up near the prow. Someone was moving around inside. Three more men were already on the beach. My stomach sank. Fear made my heart pound. Our turtle was down there somewhere.

From our hiding spot, we saw a grove of trees surrounding the half-moon beach. If we stayed in the patch of trees, we could get a lot closer without being seen. Staying low, we moved downhill and angled left, toward a stand of young trees. I sighed in relief as we slipped into the safety of their cover. The trees were young, no bigger around than Hector's skinny legs. They'd be no good to hide behind. But there were a lot of them, and in the dark, they made pretty decent cover. I breathed in the comforting smell of sweet forest scents: a mixture of flowers, rich soil, and leaves. I moved carefully, trying not to step on twigs. We moved as close as we dared, hid in some bushes, and spied out.

The fishing boat waited out in the cove, farther away than it had appeared when I first saw it. The poachers had used a Zodiac, a fast, inflatable boat, to get to shore. They left it in plain sight by the water. I spotted four men in total: three men by their flashlight beams, plus the fourth waiting on the fishing boat. We probably could have found them even without their lights. Those guys sure made a lot of noise.

Two men passed by, not twenty feet away from us. I ducked and hid my face. That trick came from playing nighttime hide-and-seek in our old neighborhood in Puerto Rico. Sometimes, all you'd see of a person hiding in the dark was a bit of starlight gleaming off an eye. I kept my face down until the men had passed.

Then Hector tugged on my sleeve and pointed. A dark, hulking shape lay on the pale beach. The rustle of moving sand told me the mother turtle was here, digging a nest, or covering up a finished one, I couldn't tell which. Her flippers churned. My mind raced as the flashlight beams came closer to her. The turtle stopped flipping sand. Her dome-shaped shadow began to inch toward the water.

*Faster!* I wanted to scream at her. *Faster!* But sea turtles moved slowly on land.

Running feet pounded down the beach.

"Mark the nest, Jason!" a man called. "We'll come back for the eggs. Who's got the net? Catch that thing before it gets away."

I knew that voice. Bobby!

Shadowy forms surrounded our turtle. I glimpsed the net being tossed over her. Danny gasped. Emily grabbed Hector's arm to keep him from running out there.

I stood and pulled my phone from my pocket. "I've got to get this video. You guys, stay here. Be safe."

"Wh—" Hector tried to say something but the sound got cut off as Danny put his hand over my brother's mouth.

I darted through the dark trees and bushes, silent as a shadow, slowing only to pull out my phone and open the camera app. The screen seemed to light up the whole forest. I hid the phone in the pocket of my black jacket and snuck closer. Tingles of nervous energy filled my body. I was a secret agent for real. It was awesome. Awesomely terrifying.

# The Night Mission, Part 3

The three men surrounded the turtle. Working together, they managed to flip the turtle onto her back. She kicked helplessly, unable to turn herself over again.

My heart raced. I had to get the video without being seen, and get it to Dr. Angela. Then I had to hurry back to the others. I tried to take a picture, but I was too far away. The picture was too dark. The poachers' faces had to show, or it was no good.

I gripped the phone between my damp palms and forced my feet closer. My breath sounded loud in my ears. The men heaved on the net. The turtle let out a croak.

I leaped from the woods, camera raised, and hit the button. I messed up, and the flash went off! Three blinding strobe lights blinked in quick succession. I got three perfect shots, showing their startled faces, their hands holding our turtle in the net, everything.

I ran.

"Stop that kid! Get her camera!" Bobby yelled.

Heavy boots crashed through the brush behind me. Electric tingles of terror shot through my body. Arms and legs pumping, I zigzagged up the hill, dodging bushes and trees. I could hear one man fall behind. Another man tripped and fell with a grunt.

Emily popped out of a bush beside me, hand out. I had no idea where she came from, but at that point I didn't care. I slapped my phone into her palm. We split up and ran in opposite directions. One man was still following me. I sped up. I guess he never even saw Emily. And that meant he couldn't have known that my phone wasn't with me anymore!

I don't think the poacher saw in the dark as well as I did. I jumped mud puddles that splashed under his big feet. I ducked under low branches that scratched his face. Roots trailed along the ground, tangling his boots. A rush of adrenaline filled my body. He couldn't catch me!

Suddenly, I heard a loud crack behind me. I turned and saw Bobby hit the ground hard. He groaned, clutching his leg. A slender shadow stood behind him, holding a long stick. Hector! He dropped the stick and started running toward me.

"Keep going!" Hector yelled to me.

I slowed my pace until he caught up.

"Tried to . . . trip him," he gasped as we dashed up a wooded slope.

No way could Bobby catch us after that! As we made our way farther inland, young trees gave way to older ones, mostly live oak and flowering dogwood. Danny's fake owl hoot came from the branches of a huge oak.

Hector and I followed the sound and climbed up after him. The bark felt rough and reassuring under my hands, and leaves cloaked us in ominous shadows. Nobody would see us up there. Hector tucked himself safely in a fork of the tree, about thirty feet off the ground. I straddled a thick, horizontal branch below Danny and hung on.

Emily's owl hoot came from a nearby tree. I hoped she still had my phone. Then Danny prodded my elbow and silently slipped something smooth into my hand. Emily had passed it to him! I was relieved. Those guys didn't know who to chase.

I texted Dr. Angela the pictures of the poachers and the turtle in the net. Under it, I added the caption: *"EMERGENCY. TURTLE POACHERS CAPTURED MOTHER LEATHERBACK."* Luckily, I'd been the navigator, so I had our GPS coordinates right there on the phone. I copied those in and hit "Send."

Just in case Dr. Angela didn't get the message, I sent pictures of the poachers to Jennifer and Janey too. I added a quick note with our location and a plea for them to send help, to call the police, the park rangers—anybody!

"I should call the police too," I whispered.

Hector's soft voice barely carried to my ear. "Someone's coming. They'll hear you."

Slow, quiet footfalls approached our tree. I turned my phone screen off, pocketed it, and clung to the branch with both hands. I inhaled as I heard the strangers come closer.

*Can you text 911?* I wondered. I was afraid to try. I took some comfort in the thought that I had already sent out the pictures. No matter what happened, at least the evidence was out there.

The footsteps passed our tree and kept on going. I couldn't believe it! I let out my breath in a whoosh.

We needed to get down there and save that turtle.

Hector read my mind. "Turtle Defenders, unite!" he softly called to the Squad.

Hector, Danny, Emily, and I made our way down from our hiding spots in the trees. Below, the full moon lit the cove in a silver glow. There was only one man left on the beach. There was a man still waiting in the getaway boat in the cove, and I'm not sure where Bobby and Jason were. Still, this man wasn't going to make much progress dragging the turtle alone. Mainly because she was seven feet long and weighed probably three quarters of a ton. I'm also not sure what they planned to do with her; wouldn't that inflatable boat have sunk with her in it? Maybe they didn't know how heavy leatherback turtles are.

We snuck down to the beach, taking a detour around the place where Hector had tripped Bobby. We weren't taking any chances. We peeked out from the trees to get a better view. Our turtle lay on her back, tangled in a net. Her flippers waved. Whew! She was still alive.

Danny stepped out of the bushes and let the poacher on the shore see him. The man jumped to his feet. He was a young guy with black, slicked-back hair, wearing tight jeans and pointy-toed cowboy boots. He had a thin mustache, and a heavy gold chain with a dollar sign hung around his neck.

"Do you know that sea turtles are an endangered species?" Danny asked. "They're protected. You could go to prison for this."

"It's none of your business, kid," the poacher snarled.

"I think it *is* my business," Danny said. I could see that Danny was about the same height as the man.

The poacher was so busy arguing with Danny, he didn't see me, Hector, and Emily slip behind him and run for the Zodiac. Working together, we pushed the inflatable boat off the beach and into the surf. The tide was going out. Slowly, the boat began to drift out to sea. I stepped into the water, knee deep, to give it one last shove. That would make it a lot harder for the poachers to get away. Hector and I shared a triumphant grin, and Emily and I softly high-fived each other.

The captain of the fishing boat saw us. He stepped out on deck and started yelling at us. The poacher on the beach spun around so fast, his necklace flew up, and the gold dollar sign hit him in the ear. He slapped a hand to the side of his head and sucked in air through his teeth. When he saw the inflatable boat disappearing out to sea, he cursed. The captain of the fishing boat motored after the inflatable, leaving us all behind.

"You rotten kids!" the poacher on the beach yelled. He hiked up his pants and chased us, alligator-skin cowboy boots slipping and sliding on the sand.

Emily, Hector, and I sprinted away, circled back, and ran to Danny.

The poacher couldn't find his footing and fell into the mud, cursing as he did.

The trapped turtle let out a weak grunt and a sigh of air through her nostrils. I hurried over to her, with Hector right behind me. We untangled the net and threw it off, but she was still upside down. We slid our hands under her leathery sides and lifted with all our might. All we did was rock her. We called for Danny and Emily to help us. We couldn't lift her alone.

They moved toward us, but the fallen poacher had righted himself and shadowed them. They didn't dare turn their back on the guy.

Hector astonished me when he spoke to the poacher. "Sir? Will you give us a hand here? Help us flip over this turtle so she can get back to the water."

The poacher snorted a laugh.

Hector told him the cops were coming. He promised the poacher the cops would go easier on him if he helped us. My brother sounded so convincing, I almost forgot he had no authority over the police.

The man looked around, scanning the night-black water of the cove. Nobody was there.

I told the man I had texted his picture to the police already. That wasn't strictly true, but I'm sure Dr. Angela or Janey and Jennifer would send it in for me.

Moonlight caught a sheen of sweat on the poacher's upper lip. "This isn't worth it. I'm outta here." He hurried away, slipping on the sand in those silly boots.

He was heading straight into the swamp. We let him go. The poacher was on his own with the alligators and the snakes. Good luck to him.

All of us rushed over to the upside-down turtle. All together, we were like superheroes. Using pieces of driftwood as a lever, we managed to heave the heavy turtle right-side-up again. The transmitter on her back looked undamaged. The antenna wasn't even broken. I expected her to flee back to the sea, but she didn't move.

"Guys, let's give her some space," I said. "She just had a really bad experience with humans. Maybe she'll go back to sea if we back off."

So we all backed away to the edge of the beach. In a minute, the turtle scooted a few inches closer to the sea. Then she stopped again and lay there, a huge black shadow against starlit sand.

"We'll stand guard over her until she goes back to the ocean," Hector declared. He folded his arms and braced his feet wide apart in a pose right off the cover of a comic book.

I copied Hector's heroic pose, chin held high, until he saw me and laughed. "We're a team. Turtle Defenders," I said.

"Turtle Defenders!" Emily and Danny echoed.

"Aw. Ain't that cute," said a cold voice from behind me.

We whirled. Bobby stepped closer to us. He had piercing gray eyes, a narrow face, and deep hollows under his cheekbones. His friend Jason—the big guy with that same Panthers cap—stood behind him. The urban cowboy with the gold dollar sign around his neck must have really run off—he was nowhere in sight. The two poachers split up and hemmed us in. I got ready to run, but if we did, they'd get the turtle! I backed up a few feet. My mind raced, wondering what to do.

Suddenly, a helicopter zoomed overhead, flying low. The loud thrumming of the rotors cut off all conversation. White print spelled out the word POLICE on the tail. I grabbed my flashlight out of my pocket, switched it on, and waved it like crazy. I jumped up and down, yelling my head off.

# The Night Mission, Part 4
## (The Rescue)

The helicopter circled and came back, shining a bright spotlight down on us. It hovered overhead, rotors thrumming, so close that I felt the vibrations in my chest. A ladder unrolled out of its side. I squinted against the bright light. Wow! I sure was glad those guys were on our side.

"Cops! Get to the boat!" Bobby roared. He sprinted toward the surf.

His friend followed, but the two of them straggled to a halt and gazed out over the water. The Zodiac was gone, and along with it, the big fishing boat that had

been waiting for them in the cove. The poachers took off toward the south, running along the beach.

Two police officers had made their way off the helicopter and ran to intercept the poachers. "Police! Stop right there!" one of them shouted.

I'm not even sure where they came from, but I couldn't believe our plan was working!

The poachers turned around and came running north again, along the water, with blue-uniformed police officers chasing them. A pack of green-suited park rangers came from the other direction. The criminals got trapped between waves of green and blue. In seconds, the poachers were caught. The police put them facedown on the sand and handcuffed their hands behind their backs.

Just then, a familiar white catamaran slid into the cove. The Wildlife Rehabilitation Clinic's black turtle logo was painted on the prow. Dr. Angela, in blue surgical scrubs, splashed to shore. She was followed by other vets and biologists and Tío Gustavo! Tío ran to us and pulled Hector and me into a big bear hug.

"What were you two THINKING?! Your mother will have my head when she wakes up," he said.

"I know," I said after I was released from his grip. "I'm sorry."

Dr. Angela interrupted by putting her hand on his back. "They saved a turtle's life tonight, Gus."

"I know Angie, but—" Tío started to protest.

"But look at these kids," she said to him, soothingly. "They did the right thing. When they got in over their heads, they called for backup."

"Heart rate is a little high, but nothing dangerous," a biologist (Brian, I think?) called from where he was examining our turtle.

"See?" Dr. Angela said. She turned to the Squad. "I think the turtle will be fine."

But Tío wasn't done lecturing. His eyes were wide. "I saw the photos you sent to Dr. Angela. Clarita, you got really close to those guys. They're criminals. That was incredibly dangerous."

I needed to stand up for myself. "I had to," I said. "If they weren't recognizable, it was no good as evidence."

"Shh, everyone," Hector whispered. "Look!"

Hector pointed at the mother turtle, who was finally moving toward the water.

*Tío and Dr. Angela stood, heads close together, watching her. Qué romántico. I nudged Hector, and we both smiled.*

*Using both front flippers together, the mother leatherback scooted toward the water. The Turtle Defenders lined up and watched her go. I smiled as she disappeared into the waves. Beside me, Hector crossed his arms over his torn Superman T-shirt and sniffled. We'd done it. We had saved her!*

*Dawn painted the eastern horizon a deep, lovely blue. I couldn't believe we'd been out all night! In the first gray light of morning, I saw that Emily was covered in mud. Danny had scratches on his face. And Hector had dark shadows under his eyes and a bruise that darkened one cheekbone.*

*"You were brave tonight, hermanito," I said to Hector. "You saved me when that guy was chasing me." I swung an imaginary stick at knee level. "Pow!"*

*Hector grinned. "You were brave too. Your knees are all scraped up." Then he smiled. "Mamá's gonna lose her mind when she sees us."*

*I shrugged. "Yeah. Well, we'll just have to tell her how I'm a secret agent now. A little blood is part of the job."*

"I'm no secret agent. I'm a superhero," Hector said. He puffed out his narrow chest, showing off the Superman logo. We both cracked up laughing.

I glanced up and saw Tío looking at us. He winced. "Look at you kids. What am I gonna tell your mother?" (Even though he'd JUST said that five minutes ago.)

"Even though you did something dangerous, you kept this turtle safe. I wish everyone cared as much as you do about these animals," Dr. Angela said. "I think you've all earned Science Squad Animal Protector badges!"

Emily and Danny gave each other high fives, and Hector and I hugged.

Dr. Angela suggested we all go out for breakfast.

Tío suggested the Oceanside Café. Then he whispered an apology to "Angie" for taking kids along on their first date. Hector overheard that and pretended to gag. All the kids giggled.

Behind Tío's back, I gave Dr. Angela the thumbs-up sign. She saw me and smiled.

We had to get our gear first. Back at the tent, Emily, Danny, Hector, and I took turns changing into clean clothes and then splashed water on our faces and hands. I shook my head like a wet dog, scattering droplets of water everywhere.

"There. Do I look normal now?" I asked Hector.

Hector smirked. "Did you ever?"

I giggled. Scratches, bruises, and mosquito bites covered our skin. We'd been on an incredible adventure, and it showed.

Hector pulled a big, foil-wrapped chocolate bar out of his duffel bag. My mouth watered just looking at it. To my surprise, he offered some to me. And he didn't just give me a section or two. He broke it in half! That was when I knew we really were a team. I've never tasted something so delicious in my life.

Brian offered the Science Squad a ride home on the big, comfortable catamaran. Tío and Dr. Angela went together in his skiff. He held her hand as he helped her on board. She didn't seem to mind.

As we headed south toward home, Emily and I laid down on the padded benches along the rail. Hector and Danny stretched out on the opposite side and instantly passed out. A beautiful sunrise lit the clouds with peach and pink and gold.

It wasn't long before the drone of the motor and the slow rise and fall of the waves lulled me to sleep too.

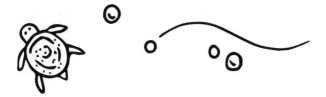

# Celebrity Superheroes

I bolted upright to someone standing over me. We were back. The catamaran floated in its usual slip in the harbor. Why had no one woken me?

A jowly white-haired police officer looked down at me, rubbing his wrinkly, sunburned neck with one hand. He knew my name and didn't look threatening. I yawned and looked around. Sunlight blazed down from high overhead. I'd slept through the whole trip, and then some. Hector stood on the pier, talking with Tío and Dr. Angela. Emily and Danny were gone, along with their packs. Their parents had probably picked them up. So much for breakfast together. Everyone had let me sleep while they'd talked to cops and park rangers. Now it was my turn.

The police officer took a seat next to me and balanced his pen and paper on one knee. He went over the story about the poachers attempting to catch the sea turtle. Mostly, he seemed to want me to say yes *or no to the facts he listed. Yes, I was sure it was a leatherback. I knew it for sure because I'm in Science Squad. Yes, I knew leatherbacks were an endangered species. Yes, I felt threatened by the poachers, who chased me. No, they didn't catch me. I was faster. I left out the part about Hector whacking that man in the knee with a stick. Ha!*

*The police officer took lots of notes. Then he asked a question that I wasn't sure how to answer: What made us decide to interfere with the hunt?*

*I wanted to tell him it was illegal. That those poachers caught an endangered animal, a rare leatherback sea turtle. But the police officer knew all that. I thought about it and then said that interfering with the hunt was scary. Super scary. I'd probably have nightmares about turtle poachers. But letting them kill her would have been worse. What if leatherbacks went extinct? What if one of the last breeding females got killed on my home state, and I did nothing about it? I am only twelve. But I knew I'd remember* that for the rest of my life. I had to blink back tears when I got done telling him.

The police officer got quiet. He looked at me funny, and I wondered what he was thinking. Then he asked me if I thought protecting endangered animals was my responsibility. I said I thought it was EVERYONE'S responsibility. I just did my part, and so did my friends. Looking back, I hope I wasn't being disrespectful when I said that. I wasn't trying to be. I was just speaking the truth.

My stomach growled. I was starving and just wanted to eat. I tried to sum it up for him. I told him a crime was committed. He had evidence, and he had witnesses.

"Yes, you are right about that," the police officer said, shaking his head. Then, a little more softly, "Times sure do change. We used to make turtle soup when I was a kid."

I shuddered. He was right. Times *did* change.

Glancing over the police officer's shoulder, I saw Hector, Tío, and Dr. Angela had come up behind the officer and were listening in. Dr. Angela caught my eye and gave me an encouraging nod. I stood, hoping we were done.

"Oh, wait. One more thing," the officer said. "Dispatch got at least fifty calls last night from a couple kids. The Chen sisters. They kept on bugging us until we told 'em we'd send out patrols to check on you. They gave us your names. What was that about?"

I grinned and told him that Jennifer and Janey were our friends from Science Squad. We cared about each other and about nature too. Our chapter was based here, but there were Science Squad kids all over the world. That reminded me, I needed to let them know we were okay. The police officer said they had told Jennifer and Janey that already. He said it was the only way to get them to stop calling—especially the younger one. I laughed. Being annoying WAS Janey's superpower. At that moment, I loved her for it.

The officer shook my hand and thanked me for my time. He walked down the dock, muttering to himself, "Endangered, huh? No more turtle soup. That's a shame."

I stepped toward Hector, Tío, and Dr. Angela. I secretly hoped Dr. Angela might become part of our family too, if it worked out between her and Tío. What a cool aunt she'd be, with a giant white catamaran to take us out in. Okay, I know even thinking that was a little selfish. But I couldn't help it.

"Should we grab some breakfast then?" Tío asked. "I've called your mother, and she'll be meeting us there." Tío eyed Hector and me.

"Not so fast," Dr. Angela said and then turned toward me. "The way you educated that officer on the plight of sea turtles was commendable. Educating a person in authority isn't easy, but you did so clearly and politely."

WHAT?! I wasn't *trying* to educate him. I was just trying to defend the sea turtles, like the Squad and I had vowed to do.

Dr. Angela went on, "Now that police officer will press charges against those poachers."

"Clarita schooled a cop," Hector giggled.

I didn't mind if he laughed at me. At that point, my stomach had my attention. I would have done just about anything for a plate of pancakes, even if I was dreading seeing Mamá there. I was going to be grounded until I was thirty!

Tío pressed his lips together. "I wouldn't be laughing, Hector. What you kids did was dangerous. It was irresponsible to run away. I trusted you two—and your friends. But you broke that trust." He shook his head and took a breath before he said one more thing. "Your mother saw the rescue on the news."

We stood in silence as that sank in a bit. Hector and I looked at each other. We must have been thinking the same thing: Mamá had to be freaking out.

Apparently, the TV news story had been very positive. It didn't show our pictures or mention our names, but my mom was pretty sharp and put two and two together. (Maybe I get my secret agent skills from her?) It was just a feel-good story about local kids doing good. They even showed the pictures I had taken of the poachers with the turtle in the net. But I don't think Mamá will be able to look past the fact that we'd snuck out to catch some

poachers. Even if we were only trying to defend the sea turtles.

Tío looked down and ran his hand through his hair. "Um, Clarita? Your mother . . . somehow . . . got the impression that the telephoto on your new phone is really great."

I let that sink in. "Oh. Right! The telephoto is excellent. I took those pictures from a safe distance. Very safe. Very far away. That telephoto magnified everything."

Hector snorted, and then we both busted up laughing. Tío put his face in his palm.

As I suspected, the talking-to we got from Mamá in the Café's parking lot was epic. There were a lot of "Clarita Rosita Santiago Romeros" thrown around, and, as suspected, Hector and I are both grounded AGAIN. But I'm okay with that. We did save that turtle, after all, didn't we? It was worth it.

When we got home, Tío and I went on a walk along the beach. I told him everything that had happened with the poachers, even the scary parts. He was obviously mad at us for sneaking off, but I still think a little bit of him actually admired what we did. It felt good to get the whole story off my chest.

I can't stay awake any longer. That was a long night. Maybe it's time for a nap.

ZZZZzzzzzz

# Catch Up

Hector and I got un-grounded yesterday. You would think with our punishment of the century, I would have written in here more, but I was having too much fun! Honestly, it wasn't near the punishment Mamá seemed to think it was. I didn't point that out. The thing is, Mamá didn't want us watching too much TV. So her rule didn't limit us from going outside, at least not to the beach right outside our door. We couldn't have friends over or go to their houses, but that was okay. Hector and I have become pretty good pals. We learned to surf together! Mr. Carter gave us a couple old surfboards. I'm stronger, so I paddle faster, but Hector has better balance. I've wiped out and gotten churned under waves more times than I can count, but I'm getting better. I rode a wave all the way to the beach yesterday!

With all the excitement about the turtles, I didn't think we'd have time for much fun this summer. But the last few weeks had been great. That's good because there's only one more month of summer before school starts. I try not to think about it, but maybe now that I have the Squad for friends, school won't be so lonely this year.

Angela is Tío's girlfriend now, and she spends a lot of time at our house. I don't call her Dr. Angela anymore, now that she's practically family.

# Got My Badge!

Today might have been the very best day of the summer! Danny, Emily, Hector, and I received our Animal Protector badges at a ceremony at the Wildlife Rehabilitation Clinic this evening. Mamá was so proud. She bought me a new white dress and matching sandals for the event. Hector got a suit, but he wore it with flip-flops and without a tie. When I saw what he had on under his suit jacket, I gave him a thumbs-up. He had on a brand-new Superman T-shirt! His old one got torn up when we were out in the salt marsh on real-life hero business.

The ceremony happened outside on the back deck of the Clinic, where they keep injured sea turtles. They set up rows of chairs between the kiddie pools, so sea turtles swam all around us. A roof covered the porch, but the sides were open, so we looked out on the ocean. Someone had decorated the space with streamers and little cloth flags.

Angela got up in front and made a speech about some of the stuff the Science Squad had done to protect the turtles. She told how we'd defended the eggs and "witnessed" some poachers trying to kill a turtle. Then we "called the authorities." That's not *quite* the way it happened. But I was relieved that Angela left out the scary stuff. I'm sure Tío told her all about everything, but I didn't want the whole world to know what we went through. It made me happy that Angela understood that without being told. Plus, I'm still not sure if everything we did was legal, even if those poachers were criminals. Normally, stuff like untying somebody's boat and pushing it out to sea is, um, "frowned upon," as Mamá would say.

Angela called each of us up in front of the crowd and gave us our Animal Protector badges. I pinned mine to my dress. People clapped and cheered. A pretty good-sized crowd showed up, with Clinic people, wealthy donors, and even two new Science Squad kids I'd never seen before. They were brown-haired twin sisters, about Hector's age. They stared at me, open-mouthed, like I was some kind of celebrity. When I said hi, they blushed like crazy and didn't answer.

After we got our awards, there was a reception on the deck with cookies and punch. Hector took Rose and Ruby (the new Science Squad girls!) around the turtle tanks. They didn't seem shy around him. I overheard Hector telling them what injury each turtle was in the hospital for. He remembered everything we'd learned on our first tour there. I was happy to see that.

Angela came to sit next to me. "So, big day today," she said.

"Yeah, I guess it is," I said.

"Hopefully the heroic work you kids did will help discourage poaching around here and inspire others to watch out for the turtles and their nests," she said.

I agreed. I definitely felt better knowing all those poachers were facing big fines and possibly even jail time. Well, all of them except the urban cowboy—that guy with the alligator-skin cowboy boots and the big gold dollar sign around his neck. He ran into the swamp alone, so the police didn't get him when they caught the others. Hopefully, they'd catch up with him eventually.

It was nice sitting there and talking with Angela. She was starting to feel more like a big sister than our Science Squad mentor.

*I glanced up when a long shadow fell across our table. That same white-haired cop was there—the man who'd questioned me after our adventure.*

*"What are you doing here?" I blurted. "Um, I'm sorry, you're very welcome at the party. I just, uh . . . hope I'm not in trouble." Boy, I really put my foot in my mouth there. I felt the hot blush creep up my cheeks to my hairline.*

*Angela explained that Officer Sanders had started volunteering at the Clinic, right after he'd interviewed me. And he had made a very generous donation to the Wildlife Rehabilitation Clinic. She said that something got him interested in sea turtle conservation, and smiled at me.*

*Officer Sanders told us he was getting ready to retire, and he "wanted something to keep me busy, now that I can't be making turtle soup anymore." Then he winked, so I realized he was joking. Then he said, "But I have some news that I think you'll be happy to hear, Clarita."*

*He told us that the last poacher—the urban cowboy— had crawled out of the swamp last night. He wasn't in the best of shape. He was hungry and thirsty, with a* million mosquito bites. Somebody'd been breaking into vacation cabins in the area, so the police had been on the lookout for him.

Angela let out a relieved sigh. "That's great news," she said.

I agreed. It was the best news I'd had all week!

It took forever to thank everyone, say goodbye, and leave the Clinic. Hector and I danced with excitement as we walked out to our car. What a great night!

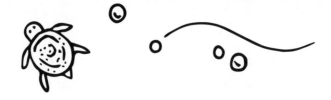

# The Baby Turtles
# Are Coming!

Great news! The Clinic biologists who have been monitoring the turtle nest think the eggs will hatch soon. Maybe even tonight!

Mamá let us invite the whole Science Squad over tonight to (hopefully) watch the baby turtles hatch. Everyone knew where we lived except for Rose and Ruby. Mamá called their parents and made sure they were invited too. I love that about her. She never wants anyone to feel left out.

But the hatchlings aren't here. Not yet, anyway. (I just checked.) That's good. With the sun still up, seagulls would gobble them right up. I'll write all about the hatching later. People are starting to arrive, and I have to go keep my eye on that nest!

# Turtle Hatching, Part 1

I cannot BELIEVE how many people showed up for our party tonight. The entire Science Squad came—and their parents. We haven't had this many people in our tiny house since we came from Puerto Rico! It was nice.

We tried to keep as many people in the house as we could. We didn't want the beach to be too noisy or bright. That might confuse the hatchlings. But it was hopeless trying to keep that many people indoors on a beautiful summer night. The best that we could hope for was that everyone would quiet down and stay out of the way when the eggs were hatching.

Angela and Brian kept an eye on the nest, and I checked on them every so often. At one point, Angela and Brian were sitting in the sand near the nest. Brian had some big headphones on and was listening intently. Angela raised a questioning eyebrow at him. He pulled off his headphones and his face split into a big grin. "I hear them!"

Brian held out the headphones to me. "Listen. They're communication signals."

I slipped on the headphones and stood still, eyes closed. Soft croaks, chirps, and grunts came through, first one or two, then a whole symphony of them. They were baby turtle noises! I never knew they made noise.

"Are they hatching under the sand?" I asked anxiously. "Do we need to dig them out?"

Brian said that when baby leatherbacks are almost ready to hatch, they talk to each other from inside their eggshells. That way, predators can't eat all the hatchlings. These are some other things he told me:

# TURTLE SOUNDS

1. People used to think turtles were deaf and mute because they so rarely made noise. But they're not.

2. In the egg, hatchlings make over 300 unique sounds! They call to one another, not to their mother. She is gone by then.

3. Scientists believe baby turtles coordinate hatching with calls, so they know to all come out of their eggs at once.

4. So far, we know of forty-seven species of turtles that make sounds.

5. Scientists are still learning what all the sounds mean. Some noises communicate social standing, like which turtles are bosses over which.

6. Other sounds announce when a turtle might be ready to mate.

I pressed the headphones over my ears with both hands and listened again. We had a lot of live babies in that nest!

I pulled off the headphones and ran to get the rest of the Squad. Hector listened first. His eyes lit up when he heard the babies. Then he closed his eyes and listened for a long time. After everything we'd gone through to keep those eggs alive, those little chirps and grunts meant a lot to us.

After Hector, Danny wanted to listen too. Soon, everyone on the Science Squad took a turn listening.

Chatter broke out among the adults, and Hector and I shushed them. There had to be twenty people out back. It was great to see how many people cared about sea turtles. Even though Angela tried to limit how many people came, we still recognized donors, volunteers, and veterinarians from the Clinic.

Hector, Emily, Danny, and I (go Turtle Defenders!) took it upon ourselves to keep the group in order. We needed to make sure all the lights were turned off when the hatchlings began to emerge. Turtle hatchlings move toward light, and the light we wanted them to move toward was the moonlight reflecting off the ocean. NOT the porch light or a bonfire or anything else. That would get them going in the wrong direction. We also wanted everyone to stay quiet and keep off the sand around the nest.

Angela told us it would be a late night if we wanted to stay up and watch the hatching. And we *did* want to! Mamá said we could take as many pillows and blankets as we needed from the house. I guess we got that beach campout with the Science Squad after all. Ha!

Hector and I ran inside and raided the camping closet. He wanted to set up the tent, so Danny and I lugged that out for him. Just for fun, we brought sleeping bags and battery-powered lanterns outside too. Our "camp" was only about twenty feet off the foot of the stairs, close to the turtle nest but not in the hatchlings' path to the water. With Emily's and Danny's help, we set up the tent, crawled inside, and unrolled our sleeping bags.

In the back of the tent, Emily pulled down the flap that covered the screened-in window. A fresh sea breeze streamed through. The salty sea air smelled good. Like home.

Once the tent was all set, Emily, Danny, Hector, and I ran around the beach, chasing little waves toward the ocean and then running away as the surf came back in. We all ended up with wet feet, but it was warm so we didn't mind.

Tío fired up the grill (but in the driveway—so it wasn't near the turtle nest). Wonderful smells of steak and barbeque chicken filled the air. Our kitchen overflowed with Science Squad parents and people from the Clinic. We were finally making friends in North Carolina.

# A Note about Noise Pollution:

When sea turtles are ready to hatch, it is very important to minimize as much noise pollution as possible. I had heard of air pollution before but never noise pollution. The idea is that the baby turtles needed to be able to HEAR each other. Noise pollution gets in the way of that.

Noise pollution includes any loud noises created by people and machines—even nice music! I guess nature was meant to be fairly quiet. The loudest sounds should be bird songs or coyote howls. When humans started running engines, the whole world got louder. The rumble of ships or highway traffic can drown out the noises animals make when they talk to each other. If the baby turtles couldn't hear each other from inside their eggs, they probably wouldn't hatch all at once. And if only a few came out at a time, predators would get them all! The Turtle Defenders wouldn't let that happen. Not on our watch!

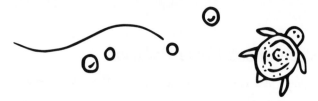

# Turtle Hatching, Part 2

Tío is a grill master, and soon, every guest had a plate. The grown-ups sat on folding chairs on the back porch of our little wooden house. They didn't seem to mind that our place wasn't big or that it needed a coat of paint. Most of the Science Squad kids sat on big beach towels outside the open door of our tent. The sun dropped behind our house, leaving us in soothing shade. We all munched happily.

Sitting with my brother and my new best friends, I finally felt like I belonged. Then I noticed some other kids wandering around alone. Well, not exactly alone. Rose and Ruby were sitting with the grown-ups on the porch. Carl and Trent were together too, over by the food table. Honestly, I wasn't even sure how they'd found out about the party.

I wasn't going to ask those boys to leave though. I knew how it felt to be left out. I still remembered what that felt like when I'd first moved here. The new kid, the one with no friends. I'd never want anyone else to feel that way.

I felt shy about going over to talk to them. Those boys didn't talk to or make eye contact with anyone. All they did was stare at their plates and eat really fast, like we might change our minds and send them away. It must have felt weird being here with a bunch of turtle defenders when, at one point, they had been accomplices to a poacher. To be fair, they hadn't known they were helping out a poacher at the time, but the reality is that they had. So I can imagine how hard coming to this party must have been for them. They were brave to show up here at all, when you look at it that way.

I nudged Hector and twitched my chin toward Rose and Ruby. He got the idea, jumped up, and went to talk to them.

I made myself stand up too. My feet felt heavy as I walked over to Trent and Carl. I could feel myself blushing. I smiled and said hi to Carl. I introduced myself to Trent and invited them both to come play cards with us. At first, they didn't answer.

I stood still, feeling more and more uncomfortable, while nobody said anything. Then I added that we had cookies in the tent. Did they like chocolate cookies with creamy white filling? Yes! That did it. They followed me back to sit in our circle with us. The Science Squad kids smiled at them, said hi, and went back to chattering about baby turtles.

Janey thought she'd keep a hatchling as a pet. It could live in the bathtub and eat soap. That was ridiculous, and Jennifer told her so. I told her so too. Nobody lived on soap. You'd get sick and throw up bubbles! Besides, sea turtles needed to be free.

Carl and Trent smiled a little at Janey's silliness, but mostly they stared at the sand. They didn't say much. I kept putting cookies into their hands, which seemed to help some. After all, people don't give you cookies unless they like you. Whenever I talked, I tried to include them too. At least they seemed excited to see the turtles hatch.

"The babies are going to live," Trent said to his brother. "Nobody's gonna hurt 'em. They'll swim away and be free."

"That's right," Carl said with a big grin. That smile faded when he saw me listening. He pressed his lips together and a guilty flush crept up his cheeks.

I invited Trent and Carl to stay and watch the hatching with us. We were all going to camp out, and we had extra sleeping bags and stuff if they needed it. Of course, our mother would want to talk to their mother on the phone before they could stay. I blurted that out without thinking. Carl flushed and said they lived with their father.

I bit my lip, winced, and said nothing. I shouldn't have assumed they had a mom at home. Hector and I hated it when people assumed we had a father at home, which we don't. He left a long time ago, when I was small and Hector was a baby. So you would have thought I'd know better. I felt so dumb.

Hector jumped in. He said our uncle took care of us a lot too. Then Carl relaxed a little. Hector offered to show them his comic book collection, which was all about superheroes (of course). The boys raced into the house to see them and talk to Mamá about the brothers staying over.

A little while later, Tío scratched on the door of the tent and whispered that we could go to sleep without missing anything. The adults were going to stay up and watch over the turtle nest all night long. He promised they would wake us up when the first hatchlings came out. Hector was afraid they'd forget us, but he couldn't stay awake. I saw him trying to hide his yawns.

All the kids around me are nodding off. I'm tired too, but I *had* to write this all down before I went to sleep. I'm too excited—about the turtles and about North Carolina finally feeling like home.

# Turtle Hatching, Part 3
## (It's Finally Happened!)

*Many hours later, I woke up on my own. The faint gray light of early morning filtered through the green nylon roof of the tent. Sleeping kids lay all around me. Then I remembered:* Turtles! *Did we miss them hatching?!*

*I crawled from my spot as quietly as I could, being careful not to crunch Emily, whose long legs stretched straight across the entrance. I unzipped the tent and stepped outside into the cool morning air. Blanket-wrapped adults sat in lawn chairs around the turtle nest. The orange plastic fencing had been removed and rolled up, no doubt to make way for the crawling babies. The adults' faces looked older, lined and tired. I guessed they'd been awake all night.*

*Then I noticed Brian with the headphones over his ears and a long wire disappearing into the sand below. The baby turtles hadn't hatched yet! Oh no! Nests that* hatched in daylight lost a lot of hatchlings to seagulls and crabs. I moaned. The sun was rising over the ocean, painting the clouds yellow and pink. A few seagulls flapped across the water, already on the lookout for breakfast. Those birds were not going to eat MY turtles! Not if I had anything to say about it.

Brian pulled off his headphones and said that the noises from inside the turtle eggs were changing. Nobody was sure what it meant, but the tone of their calls was definitely different.

I pointed at a spot of sand that seemed to shift on its own. "Look!" A pair of tiny flippers and a miniature turtle head poked from the sand. Its beady black eyes looked around. In seconds, the smallest, most perfect leatherback turtle I'd ever seen crawled onto the sand.

The adults got up from their chairs and quietly came over to the nest, excited to see the hatchling. Baby sea turtles always head toward light. At night, that works fine (so long as the rest of the beach is dark). The moonlight reflecting off the ocean acts like a beacon calling them home. But what would the babies do with the sun up? How would they know which way to go?

*The baby leatherback headed straight for the water. He crawled fast for a tiny guy. He was a little bit bigger than I expected, especially because he came out of an egg the size of a cue ball. I guess he must have been curled up tight in there. I followed him all the way to the waves. My head swiveled as I looked up for seagulls and down for ghost crabs. My baby made it to the waves, plunged in, and was gone.*

*I just want to stop for a minute and say I find it positively FASCINATING that baby sea turtles remember the beach they hatched on. Survivors return to that very same beach when they are old enough to breed.*

*I want all the babies from this nest to survive, but I know from my research that only about one in one thousand baby turtles make it to adulthood. That's crazy. And sad.*

*Helping hatchlings is controversial. Not everyone agrees on what is best. Some people think we should protect eggs and hatchlings of endangered species, and even raise them in captivity until they are large enough to survive in the ocean. Others believe we should let nature run its course. They worry that too much human help will make endangered animals weak.*

Angela and I talked about this before, and I came up with my own opinion. I decided that people cause a lot of problems for turtles. Our boats sometimes hit them. Our trash makes them sick. The LEAST we can do is help them out when we can.

Angela agreed with me. So that's what we did today.

"Who's ready to chase off some crabs and seagulls?!" I asked and ran to wake up the Science Squad. "Everybody, come quick. It's starting!"

Sleepy kids tumbled from the tent. Everyone was confused because the sun was up.

"Oh no!" Hector wailed. "We missed it!"

"No, we didn't," I said. "It's happening now! And we have to help them!"

"The Turtle Defenders are on the job!" Hector yelled.

The other Science Squad kids laughed but did not protest.

We quickly decided that our mission was to chase off every predator that tried to catch hatchlings as they crawled to the ocean. Seagulls were our biggest problem. They were fast and smart, and they attacked from the air. What could we do?

"Umbrellas!" Emily exclaimed.

For a second, that sounded crazy. What was she talking about? It wasn't even raining.

"Umbrellas," Emily repeated. "Do you have any umbrellas? We can open and close them at birds who dive in at the hatchlings. That will chase the birds away without hurting them."

Yes! We had three of them. Hector and Emily ran for the house, shouting, "Mamá!" and, "Umbrellas!"

The rest of us kids rushed back to check on the nest. We crouched on our heels, peering down. Another baby struggled free of the sand. He made it a few inches toward the ocean. Then a crab popped from its burrow and grabbed the baby turtle's flipper in a powerful claw. Jennifer snatched up the baby and the crab together. That stubborn crab refused to let go of its breakfast. Jennifer held them both while her sister, Janey, carefully pried the crab's claw open. The baby turtle fell to the sand and immediately headed for the ocean. It ran almost as fast as its brothers and sisters, even with a cut fin. Some instinct must have told it when it was in danger. I scooped the hungry ghost crab up and put it into an empty bucket so it couldn't make any more trouble. We would let it go free later, after the hatching.

Brian used his hands to scoop some sand off the nest. The hole below swarmed with adorable baby leatherbacks. They rushed from the nest all at once, crawling over each other in their eagerness to be free. The hatchlings were dark brown, with long, pointed fins and light-colored stripes up their backs. Those stripes would grow into the seven raised ridges adult leatherbacks all have.

Ghost crabs get their name for many reasons. One reason is they can change their color to blend in with their surroundings. Atlantic ghost crabs are sand-colored, with paler claws that are almost white. They aren't very big; their shells are about two inches across. One claw is a little bigger than the other, and both claws are very strong. They are most active at night and can quickly disappear (because they run fast). Ghost crabs are omnivores, meaning they eat both animals and plants, and have even been known to snatch up eggs in sea turtle nests.

Brian worked quickly to smooth a ramp of sand for them to crawl up, pointed right at the sea. At least one hundred babies raced for the water. More ghost crabs popped from burrows. Kids grabbed some crabs and trapped them in the bucket, but the ghost crabs were quick and hard to catch. A few of them pulled baby turtles down under the sand before we could stop them. We didn't have time for rescues. More hatchlings poured from the nest.

Seagulls circled above our heads, diving down to snatch up hatchlings. A few seagulls stole baby turtles and flew away with them. Other birds chased them, trying to steal their prizes. The harsh cries of gulls filled the air. Hector, Danny, and Emily saved a lot of turtles by flapping umbrellas at the birds. Open umbrellas blocked birds from diving on hatchlings too.

I raced up and down the beach, waving my arms at seagulls and snatching hatchlings from the claws of crabs. Every time a baby turtle made it to the waves and dived in, I counted it as a victory. We couldn't do anything about the pelicans. That day, the Eastern Brown Pelicans showed up in force. They are big, fat-bodied birds with long, pointed beaks. Under the beak is a stretchy skin pouch where they store the fish they catch.

I don't know if pelicans would go after turtles, but maybe they do. It was hard to tell. Pelicans circled gracefully over the water, just offshore. One at a time, they aimed their beaks at the ocean and dove straight down. They hit the water with a splash and came up with something wriggling in their pouch. Pelicans landed on tree branches and piers to gulp their catch, and then

they came back for more. I couldn't tell if they were catching baby turtles or the fish who came to eat the turtles. I hope it was the fish.

If any outsider were watching what was happening on the beach that morning, we all would have looked like lunatics. Everyone was racing around like crazy, snatching hatchlings away from crabs and waving our arms at seagulls. Jennifer even saved a baby turtle from the neighborhood cat, a yellow tabby with long

claws. Our bucket of crabs got fuller and fuller. Baxter came over with his tongue hanging out and a big smile on his doggy face. He loped to the water, picked up a baby leatherback, ran back to the nest, and dropped it, unhurt, right at Angela's feet! He backed up, wagging his tail like he thought she'd throw it for him.

Angela hid the turtle under one arm, protecting it from another ride in the slimy dog mouth. That was one lucky turtle! Baxter didn't bite down on it at all. Luckily, Mr. Carter came to take Baxter home.

I took the retrieved hatchling from Angela, holding it carefully in both hands. The poor thing was slick with dog spit. I ran it to the water. Squatting down, I released the baby into the waves. It swam away, looking strong and full of life.

"Good luck, little one!" I called. "Sorry about the dog germs."

I raced back up to defend more hatchlings. By then I was panting, and my legs ached. The last few baby turtles straggled from the nest. Trent and Carl stood guard over them as they crawled to the ocean. When the final two hatchlings dove into the waves, everyone whooped and high-fived in triumph.

We waited, and no more baby turtles emerged. Brian and Angela dug carefully into the nest, looking for any babies that couldn't make it out on their own. All they found were two rotten eggs that had never hatched. Angela put them up to her ear, listening for hatchling communication signals, and then wrinkled her nose at the bad smell. That was a sure sign the eggs were rotting. Angela said most nests have a few eggs that either didn't get fertilized or the turtles inside die for some reason. She handed them to Brian, who put the rotting eggs carefully in a box. They planned to clean out the insides and put the empty shells in a display case at the Wildlife Rehabilitation Clinic.

After the last baby turtle disappeared into the waves, people stretched and yawned. They thanked my mom. Some started to leave.

I saw Carl and Trent, standing off to the side of the crowd, alone (again). I went over to them.

"Have you guys ever thought about joining Science Squad?" I asked them. "We could always use more people like you."

At first, they just stared at me with shocked looks on their faces. Then Carl spoke up.

"Yeah, that sounds like it could be fun," he said. Trent agreed.

That would have been a pretty great end to a pretty great day, wouldn't it? But unfortunately, that wasn't the end. Because of, well, Janey.

# What Janey Did

After talking with Carl and Trent, I wanted a quiet moment to myself to let the early morning's events soak in. So I walked around toward the front of our house. Someone had left a cooler outside in the shade of the front porch. Thinking that maybe there was a bottle of water or juice inside, I opened the cooler. There was a pile of melting ice with a glass jar sitting atop it. Imagine my surprise when I saw something moving inside it!

I snatched up the jar. It was a baby turtle! And the lid was on! I unscrewed the lid as fast as I could. The hatchling came up for a breath of fresh air. It didn't look good. It barely kicked its fins. I stuck my finger in the water. It was cold—a lot colder than the ocean.

I hurried through the front door and down the hall, going as fast as I could without bouncing the turtle too much. "Angela! Angela, help!"

She sat at the kitchen table, sipping coffee and looking like, well, she had been up all night. I raced up to her and showed her what I'd found. Somebody had stuck a baby turtle in a jar! Angela's eyes went wide behind her cat-eye glasses. She took the jar from my hands, tested the water temperature, and winced. Just like I thought—the water was way too cold for the hatchling. We needed to warm him up right away.

"Hector, go get a bucket of seawater. Hurry!" Angela yelled.

Hector dashed outside and came back with a full bucket of seawater. He sloshed salt water up the wooden steps, but nobody minded. Angela met him on the porch. Hector, Emily, Danny, Carl, Trent, and I gathered around to watch as she gently transferred the baby leatherback into the bucket. The hatchling barely paddled.

"Do you think it's hungry?" I asked Angela.

"No," Angela said, confidently. "Hatchlings have an embryonic yolk sac inside their shell." She gently turned the turtle over and put her thumb on the hatchling's tummy, showing us where the sac must have been. "The yolk sac is absorbed before the turtle hatches. It provides them with energy for the first few days."

"So cool," Hector whispered.

"So is this baby's mom waiting for it out in the water?" Carl asked.

Hector laughed and Angela shot him a look.

"No," Angela said. "They don't need their mother. They know what foods to eat by instinct."

"So what do they eat?" Emily asked.

Danny answered that one. "I think they love jellyfish, right, Dr. A.?"

Angela smiled at Danny's nickname for her. "Yes, they do love jellyfish. And other soft-bodied animals."

The baby turtle had been in the seawater for a few minutes by now, but didn't seem to be doing any better. He still barely moved his fins.

Angela's brow creased with worry. "I think we need to get this little guy to the Clinic," she said. She looked like she needed a doctor visit herself. She was pale, and she had dark circles under her eyes. She'd been awake all night—and now this!

"I'll take you," Tío offered.

Hector, Danny, Emily, and I begged to come along too.

Suddenly, Janey burst through the back door. "Has anyone seen my turtle? I left it in the cool—" She stopped talking when she noticed the entire Squad hovering over the bucket.

Angela handled the situation, which was a good thing. Let's just say I wouldn't have been as nice as she was. I mean, YOU CAN'T KEEP A SEA TURTLE AS A PET. I already told her that. What was she thinking?!

Janey's eyes filled with tears. "I didn't mean to hurt him," she whispered.

Angela said, "We might as well turn this into a learning experience." And then invited the entire Science Squad to the Clinic.

It took three cars to fit us all. I'm in the back of Tío's car. Fuming mad at Janey.

## Notes on Hypothermia:

Why am I mad? Because our hatchling has hypothermia—he's too cold. (Thanks, Janey!) *Hypo* means low. *Thermia* is temperature. So, hypothermia equals low temperature.

If it gets even colder, it will be cold-stunned. Cold-stunned turtles are limp, and they look dead. That happens to sea turtles in the wild, when the weather turns cold very suddenly. Usually, sea turtles migrate to warmer tropical waters in the fall. But northern beaches have lots of good turtle food, like crabs, which turtles love to eat. Hungry turtles stay around late into the fall, pigging out. If the weather changes fast, they don't have time to swim south.

After sudden cold snaps, hundreds of sea turtles sometimes wash up on beaches, all at once! If they warm up slowly, they might live. Cold-stunned turtles may have to stay in turtle hospitals for two years. Really bad frostbite causes the turtles to get open sores that can get infected. Cold-stunned turtles also get joint problems and pneumonia, a lung infection. If they heal, they can be released.

## The Dos and Don'ts of What to Do If You Find a Cold-Stunned Sea Turtle

- Don't put it back in the ocean.

- Do move it above the tide line, so water doesn't cover it when the tide comes in.

- Do cover it with seaweed, and mark its location however you can.

- Do call a local aquarium, turtle hospital, or veterinarian to come pick it up.

- Don't take it indoors, and don't put it in warm water. Cold turtles need to warm up slowly.

## The ONE Thing You Must Never Forget to Do

Whatever you do, make sure you wash your hands after touching a baby turtle. And definitely don't touch your eyes or mouth! This is because some turtles and turtle eggs carry salmonella.

# Giving the Hatchling
## a Head Start

By the time we got to the Clinic, the hatchling was swimming a little. Hector and I grabbed the wire handle of the bucket and carried it inside between us. By then, the Clinic felt like a second home to me. I knew the pink-haired receptionist at the front desk. I knew every one of the displays about local animals, and I'd studied the framed photos of egrets, alligators, turtles, and snakes. The Science Squad kids looked curiously around, checking out the gift shop and the stuffed coyote by the front door. Everyone followed me and Hector as we hauled the heavy bucket of water through the museum, into the vet clinic beyond, and outside onto the back porch.

We set the bucket on a big work table. The warm, humid air under the covered porch smelled fishy from turtle food.

The whole Science Squad gathered around to watch as Angela examined her tiny patient. The baby leatherback kicked and struggled on the exam table.

"Is it a boy or girl turtle?" Jennifer asked.

"Actually, I can't tell that by just looking," Angela said. "We'd need to do a blood test."

"I hope it's a boy," Hector said.

"That would be nice," Angela mused. "But odds are, it isn't. Boy turtles are actually rare. Did you know that the temperature affects the gender ratios in hatchlings?" she asked.

"I did," I chimed in. "Warmer nests make more females, right? And climate change has warmed beaches all over the world, so most baby sea turtles are female."

"That's right, Clarita," Angela said. "But for the species to survive, we need plenty of males too. Excuse me for a moment." Angela walked away to talk to some other vets and biologists from the Clinic.

When she came back, she told us that they've decided to keep the hatchling at the turtle hospital for head-starting.

"What's that?" Hector asked.

"Head-starting is when turtles are raised in captivity until they are big enough to fight off most ocean predators," Angela said.

"How long will it stay here?" I chimed in.

"A year or two," Angela said. "Head-starting will improve this turtle's chance of survival."

"Is that what you did for that Kemp's ridley turtle we released?" I asked.

"It sure is," Angela said.

Emily wanted to know how tiny baby turtles got warm. "After all," she said, "we never see them sunning themselves on the beach."

"That's a good question," Angela said as she lifted the thermometer to check the temperature of the water. "From birth through about twelve years, young sea turtles are hard to find. Biologists call those 'the lost years' because we aren't sure where they go. There are some experiments underway, with tiny tracking devices attached to hatchlings."

The whole Science Squad got quiet. We all wanted to know what happened to our hatchlings. It turns out that, in the wild, young turtles traveled long distances. They rested on the surface of the ocean by floating

on tangled mats of seaweed. There, they could get a few inches out of the water and let the sun warm their bodies. Can you imagine how adorable that would be?

The vet techs poured seawater into a shallow pan and set it on a table near some other young turtles. Gently, Angela lifted the baby leatherback into its new home. Our hatchling looked tiny compared to the giants in the other tanks.

Angela looked up at me. "It's good you found this turtle when you did, Clarita. This hatchling is in good hands now and has a good chance of survival, thanks to you."

"You're a hero, Clarita," Hector said.

The rest of the Squad shouted their agreement.

"I blushed. It was nothing, really," I said.

Still, I can't help but think what I would look like if I really WAS a superhero. *I am no longer Clarita Rosita Santiago Romero. I am Hatchling Hero, member of the Sea Turtle Defenders.* Ha! I think I've been watching too many of Hector's superhero cartoons.

Anyway, then Janey apologized yet again. That had to be apology number seven. Or maybe nine.

Then the Squad got into a debate. They all knew that turtles returned to breed on the same beaches where they'd hatched. That was where we stopped agreeing. Jennifer and Emily thought this hatchling's home beach, right by my house, was too damaged by development. Too many people partied there. They argued that it would be better to release the hatchling on a different beach, somewhere safer, with fewer boats and people around. That way it was sure to come back to a beach that was safe.

Danny worried that the hatchling would get lost if they released it someplace else. The location of its birth had been recorded somewhere in its tiny mind. Hatchling turtles use magnetic fields to remember their home beaches. If they let the turtle go somewhere else, it would remember two places. Which one would it come back to? Would it breed at all?

I agreed with Danny. A different release beach was a bad idea. The turtle would get confused.

We took the debate to Angela. She said the hatchling had to be released where it hatched. That was why conservationists worked so hard to preserve seaside habitat and keep big oceanside hotels from going in. Danny and I whooped and high-fived. Emily and Jennifer took it well. They switched to arguing over the best ways to keep big resort chains out of our town.

Hector chimed in. "Maybe that's the next job for the Turtle Defenders," he said.

"What do you mean?" Jennifer asked.

I knew exactly what he meant. "To make sure our beach is safe for sea turtles, now and in the future," I said.

"Exactly." Hector looked at me and nodded.

The rest of the Squad quickly agreed.

Turns out, my mom was right. I've found some great friends in the Science Squad.

**Name:** leatherback sea turtle (*Dermochelys coriacea*)

**Size:** Leatherbacks are the largest species of turtle. They grow over six feet in length and dive deeper than three thousand feet in search of food.

**Migration:** Leatherbacks migrate extremely far. They travel through every ocean on Earth, except for the frigid Arctic and Antarctic. The longest recorded migration was a whopping thirteen thousand miles!

**Turtle Eggs:** Leatherback turtles lay very large clutches of eggs, with between 65 and 115 in one nest. A leatherback will lay seven to eleven nests each season. Despite the large numbers of offspring, few turtles survive. Eggs are often stolen by poachers for their rich taste, and in some developing countries, they are believed to have medicinal properties. Bright lights, noise pollution, and predators also affect the turtles making it to the ocean safely.

**Ocean Dangers:** *Even when a turtle is fully grown and out to sea, they are not free of danger. They face not only natural predators like sharks, but also human-caused hazards. The ocean is littered with garbage, such as plastic. Leatherbacks often mistake plastic bags as jellyfish and eat the bags. The plastic blocks up their digestive system and eventually causes death. Other times, leatherbacks become entangled in shrimp-fishing gear and floating garbage, and they drown.*

**How to Help Sea Turtles:** *Many fishing vessels are voluntarily switching to special gear that doesn't endanger turtles. Also, working to keep nesting beaches free of trash, light, and noise helps to protect sea turtles.*

*Many coastal cities, including those in North Carolina, have procedures and rules in place to protect sea turtles and their nests. Many of the things that the Science Squad did in this book, such as building a fence around a nest, reducing noise and light pollution on nesting beaches, and monitoring nests, are the same precautions that biologists and volunteers/citizen scientists take in real life.*

# In the Field

   Dr. Kimberly Stewart works hard to save the endangered leatherback species. Known by her friends and colleagues as the "turtle lady," she studies the leatherback population on the Caribbean island of St. Kitts.

   Because leatherbacks are so critically endangered, Dr. Stewart intervenes to rescue eggs from natural dangers like high tides and predators. She also works tirelessly to convince the island's residents not to prey on the endangered turtles. She educates them about the sicknesses spread by turtle products and presents other healthier sources of protein.

   Tagging and tracking turtles is a huge part of Dr. Stewart's work. She implants them with a painless PIT (passive integrated transponder) tag that allows scientists to track the turtle's movements and migration routes, providing a wealth of information. PIT tags are much more reliable than the external flipper tags used in the past.

   Dr. Kimberly Stewart hopes to bring the leatherback population up to safe numbers and help the people of St. Kitts achieve economic independence, without relying on the hazardous and unethical market for turtle products.

# Glossary

**catamaran** — A special kind of ship with two separate hulls connected in the middle. They come in many different sizes, from small scientific vessels to huge naval ships.

**conservationist** — Someone who works professionally to protect endangered species and prevent damage to the ecosystem.

**endangered** — When a species has few enough individuals left to be at risk of extinction, they are considered endangered. Endangered species are protected by law. The Endangered Species Act of 1973 prohibits selling products from endangered species like sea turtles or rhinos.

**fibropapillomatosis** — A virus specific to sea turtles that causes the growth of benign (non-life-threatening) tumors. The disease becomes dangerous if the tumors grow large enough to affect the turtle's vision or mobility.

**migration** — Some animals travel extremely far distances every year in search of food, mates, and places to nest. That routine travel, such as when birds go south for the winter, is called migration.

**noise pollution** — Sounds caused by humans that have an adverse effect on wildlife. For example, infant turtles rely on their sense of hearing to know when to hatch. The noises from a city confuse that sense.

**salmonella** — A common infection caused by the bacteria *Salmonella enterica*. It often contaminates uncooked chicken or pork.

**skeletochronology** — Similar to how people can tell the age of a tree by counting rings in the wood, this technique counts the growth rings in the bones of amphibians and reptiles. The bones must be artificially colored and viewed under a microscope, but they tell the precise number of years the animal lived.

## Selected Bibliography

"Life Cycle of Leatherbacks." *The Leatherback Trust*, www.leatherback.org/why-leatherbacks/life-cycle-of-leatherbacks. Accessed September 2, 2017.

"Sea Turtle Migration." *See Turtles*, www.seeturtles.org/sea-turtle-migration. Accessed September 2, 2017.

"Sea Turtle Tracking." *Sea Turtle Conservancy*, conserveturtles.org/sea-turtle-tracking. Accessed September 2, 2017.

Swinburne, Stephen R. Sea Turtle Scientist. Boston: Houghton Mifflin Harcourt, 2014.

## About the Author

Courtney Farrell is a biologist who turned her love of books into a career as an author. After publishing fourteen nonfiction books for young people, she began writing fiction. Her novel *Sacrificed* won the 2015 BTS Red Carpet Award in the YA division, and earned an Honorable Mention in that contest for Best Book of the Year. Courtney teaches Microbiology at Pikes Peak Community College.

## About the Illustrator

Arpad Olbey is an illustrator veteran and art director of his art studio in London. He works with paper, pencils, and paints, or digital high-tech equipment, depending on the project. His wish is to combine his experience and technical knowledge to deliver the best that his creativity can give to audiences.

# Runway ZomBee: A Zombie Bee Hunter's Journal

### by J. A. Watson

### Illustrated by Arpad Olbey

Hardcover ISBN: 978-1-63163-164-1

Paperback ISBN: 978-1-63163-165-8

It's summer vacation, but Raksha isn't relaxed. She's so busy hunting zombie bees for Science Squad that she hardly has time to prepare for her fashion camp runway show. Can Raksha pull it all together and prove that she can be both a fashion queen and a science geek?

# AVAILABLE NOW